# Falling for Real

## The Dare to Fall Series

## Book 2

*NEW YORK TIMES BESTSELLING AUTHOR*

# Carly Phillips

# FALLING FOR REAL

**A Dare to Fall Novella**
**One canceled date.**
**One overbooked hotel.**
**One fake boyfriend who feels way too real.**

I arrive at a family wedding expecting maid-of-honor chaos—not to share a room with Tristan Hayes, the devastatingly charming nightclub owner I've crushed on for too long.

When the hotel runs out of rooms, Tristan gives his to an elderly couple without hesitation, and I see the kind of man he is. So I offer to share my king-sized bed.

Just for the weekend. It's totally innocent.

Until my ex shows up with a date.

Suddenly Tristan's hand is on my waist, his smile lethal, and he becomes my fake boyfriend. It's temporary and perfect.

Except the chemistry *isn't* fake.

And wedding weekends don't last.

Or do they?

# CHAPTER ONE

## *Kaylee*

THE SUN IS low in the sky when I arrive at The Anchor Oasis in Key West, painting the normal light blue hue in shades of orange, pink, and purple. It's a breathtaking backdrop for the all-inclusive resort where I will spend the next four days celebrating my cousin's wedding. Ashley insisted on planning this whole event herself. I'm a corporate event planner with my best friend and partner, Rainey Dare, and I know enough that I offered to help take some of the burden off Ashley's shoulders. She declined, and I respect her decision. I'll have enough going on this weekend with my maid-of-honor responsibilities, anyway.

My hand drifts into my purse, and I assure myself the two ring boxes are exactly where they're supposed to be. At the last minute, Ashley and her fiancé decided to have their rings engraved with their initials and the wedding date, so my first official duty for the weekend was to pick them up from the jeweler and bring them with me today. It's not the most complicated task, but its importance has weighed on me ever since I placed them in my handbag.

I'm not deliberately forgetful. I was diagnosed with ADD at seventeen, just before graduation. Too late for high school but in time to help me navigate college.

Rainey never cared. She went into business with me because she knew I could handle things, and I do. I have an assistant who keeps me organized during events when I might otherwise spin out and forget something important.

Pulling up to the valet station, I grab my suitcase out of the trunk of my car and the garment bag from the back seat. I hand over my keys and stroll into the lobby, my heels clicking against the mosaic ocean-colored tile in various shades of blue. Around me, there are tons of people milling about, some of them dragging suitcases on wheels like me, ready to check in, and others are grouped together as they talk.

I join a line in front of the reception desk, where two people are checking in guests, and glance around the lobby, looking to see if I spot anyone I know. Only family members and the wedding party are arriving today. Guests will show up tomorrow evening. I don't recognize anyone, so I turn to face forward, and my breath catches in my throat at the sight of the man in front of me.

Tristan Hayes, co-owner of Midnight, an upscale nightclub in Downtown Miami with his business partners, Lucas Carras, Rainey's fiancé, and Jack Dare, Rainey's brother. Thanks to our very small world, Tristan is also in the bridal party this weekend. I'm here for the bride's side while he's here for the groom, his high school friend with whom he remains close.

In truth, Tristan is the hottest man I've ever laid eyes on. Muscular with the physique of an athlete, he's probably over six feet tall, with broad shoulders and an aura of composure that's extremely alluring. I can't help but admire his side view: the chiseled jaw, perfectly straight nose, and long, dark eyelashes that frame hazel eyes I don't have to see to envision. His hair is a deep shade of brown, trimmed short on the sides and left longer on top where it's styled purposefully messy. His entire appearance gives off an effortlessly sexy look in a way that grabs a woman's attention.

He's always had mine.

As if sensing my stare, Tristan turns, his gaze meeting mine. A smile curls his lips, showing off perfectly straight, white teeth, and my pulse skips a beat. "Hey, Kaylee. I thought *I'd* be the last one to arrive."

I chuckle. "I guess that honor belongs to me. Unless someone else shows up fashionably late." Chronic lateness is one of my flaws, at least according to my ex-boyfriend, Mark, who is also in the bridal party since he's cousins with the groom. Aware of my tendency to not be on time, I set my alarm back fifteen minutes for anything work related, but when it comes to my personal life, I'm more relaxed. I push aside thoughts of my ex being here this weekend. I'll deal with him when I have to.

The line moves, so Tristan turns and steps forward, then pivots to face me again.

"How's the club these days?" I ask, making conversation.

Though I visit Midnight with Rainey on occasion, Tristan and I are not what I'd call friends. We don't know each other well enough for that. But ever since we met, he stars in my fantasies in a way that has me flushing now. He falls under *secret crush*. Only Rainey knows my true feelings about him and she'd never share with anyone, including her fiancé.

"It's busier than ever," he says. "It was hard for Lucas and I both to get away this weekend, with Jack still in Charleston."

"Midnight's new location, right?" I've never been to South Carolina.

He nods, his gaze straying across the lobby. I turn to see Ashley and Eric locked in an embrace that turns into one very hot kiss.

"Aah, the bride and groom. Those two are sickeningly sweet," he says, but the warmth in his eyes tells me he's not being rude. Just honest.

"Are you here with …" I tap my foot as I try to remember the name of his girlfriend. I think it started with an A. "Annabelle?"

Tristan's grin grows wider, and I have to blink and break eye contact so I don't melt into a puddle at his feet. He's too good-looking for his own good.

"You mean Annika?" He laughs out loud.

I flush with embarrassment. "Right, Annika. Sorry. Is she here with you?" I ask, mentally crossing my fingers he's here alone. At least I won't be the only one.

"No, we broke up." He shrugs as if it's no big deal. "We just weren't a good fit. It's easier to be single," he says with a wink meant to charm me. And it works.

"Oh, I'm sorry to hear that." *No, I'm not.* But I push that thought away. No matter how alluring he is, I have no intention of acting on my desire for the man.

Tristan and I want very different things out of life. I'm a 'committed relationship' kind of girl, whereas he's a 'new woman on his arm every week' type of guy. Knowing that, I ogle him but have no expectations, nor have I ever tried to capture his attention. I was in a serious relationship when we met, so I ignored my attraction, which was easy enough since we only saw each other on occasional group events or when I go to the club with Rainey for a night out.

It's been a while since I saw him last. A few months ago, we were celebrating my company Golden Palm Events's completion of a big project for the Miami Thunder, an NFL team's anniversary bash that Rainey took the lead on. Tristan's girlfriend at the time, a leggy blonde, Annika, with no interest in anyone but herself, spent the whole evening with her face buried in her phone and barely said two words to any of us.

"What about you? Are you alone?" he asks.

"Not intentionally. I had a date but he's sick, so I'm flying solo this weekend, too." Maybe we can hang out together. Unless he picks up one of Ashley's pretty friends. I try not to frown at that thought.

The line *finally* moves again, and an older couple directly in front of Tristan reaches the desk. He and I continue to chat when we're interrupted by a loud, "Oh, no!"

"There must be some kind of mistake!" the older, gray-haired woman in front of him cries out, clinging to her husband's arm.

He pats her hand in a reassuring gesture. "Please check again," he says. "I made our reservation a month ago."

The brunette behind the desk sighs. "Did you use a third-party booking site?"

"Yes," the gentleman says. "Why?" he asks warily.

"I'm so sorry, but we've had an issue with reservations this weekend made through secondary sites. Unfortunately, you're not the first couple that's had this problem." She gives them a genuine, sympathetic look.

"But we booked it with a credit card," the woman says in a shaky tone. She's obviously near tears. "Can we get a different room instead?"

The employee shakes her head and shifts on her feet, her discomfort obvious. "Your card wasn't charged, but I'm so sorry. We're completely booked this weekend."

"But … it's our fiftieth wedding anniversary," the man says, putting an arm around his wife's shoulders. "And we were married here. We flew all the way here from Missouri to spend the weekend at your resort."

My heart aches for them. They had a special trip planned and now it's ruined. I wish I could do something to help them.

"You can have my room," Tristan says, as if he had the same thought, except he came up with an idea of how.

My mouth parts as the couple turns to Tristan, their wide-eyed expressions just as shocked as I feel. I can't believe he offered them his room. Where will he stay? What is he thinking?

"Oh, thank you!" the woman says, throwing her arms around Tristan.

"Are you sure?" her more reserved husband asks, but I see the hope shining in his hazy blue eyes.

"I am." Tristan grins, showing off a dimple I forgot to admire earlier. "Please, enjoy your anniversary. In fact, let me have room service bring you some champagne, as well."

Before the couple can reply, he turns to the desk again to arrange things, along with transferring his own reservation to the elderly couple. There's no hesitation, seemingly no concern there are no other rooms available at this resort. He just calmly does the right thing, the kind thing, and I'm overwhelmed by a rush of warmth for him, causing a lump to rise in my throat.

I watch in silence as the couple pause to talk to Tristan again.

Her husband steps forward, his arm extended, and they shake hands. "Thank you. You have no idea what this means to us," he says, as his wife slips under his arm and sidles up to him.

"You guys deserve to celebrate your anniversary here, where your love story began."

They finally walk away toward the elevators and

before I can say anything to Tristan, the employee behind the desk calls out, "Next!"

"That's your cue," Tristan says, bending to grab his small piece of luggage and the garment bag hanging over it.

I'm about to turn to the counter, but I hesitate as Tristan turns away from me, going where, I don't know. "Wait." I place my hand on his muscular forearm. His skin is warm, and I feel a jolt of electricity at the contact. "Where are you going?" I ask him.

He looks utterly unbothered. "I guess I'll see if there are any other hotels in the area with a room available."

"But everyone in the wedding is staying here. And the guests too." It would be inconvenient for him to be anywhere else.

"I'll make do," he assures me despite just giving away his room to strangers.

I hate the thought of him missing out on the easiness of staying at the resort because he did something nice. "You can stay with me." The words leave my mouth before I've fully thought them through. "Consider it me paying it forward. You did something nice and I'm doing the same."

He lets out an amused yet charming laugh. "I didn't do something nice for *you*, so you're not paying anything forward." His grin has me smiling back, not the slightest bit embarrassed by my mistaken phrasing.

"Well, you deserve someone to do something kind for you, so let me."

He stares at me, those hazel eyes swirling with mesmerizing shades of green and brown, wide in disbelief. "Are you sure?"

*No, I'm not.* Too late, my thoughts turn rational. Sharing my private space with a man I fantasize about is a horrible idea, but I meant the offer and I won't take it back.

"Of course I'm sure. It doesn't have to be weird. We're both here for Ashley and Eric and you need to be around if they need us just like I do." Besides, I booked a room with two double beds, thinking I was staying with my friend, Cole.

"Thanks, Kaylee. I really appreciate it." His easy smile is full of warmth.

A couple had walked around us to check in, and we wait for them to finish. Soon it's our turn to step up to the woman behind the desk. "Kaylee Martin," I tell her, handing over my license and credit card, and explain we're going to be sharing the room.

Before the receptionist can reply, a woman with two young children inserts herself too close to me and begs for just one second of the clerk's time. One second turns into almost five minutes, but she finally leaves.

"I'm so sorry," the woman tells me. "It's crazy today." She taps on her keyboard a few more times and hands me a folio with two keys for the room. I hand one to Tristan and my skin tingles with awareness where our fingers brush.

I force an unaffected smile and grab my suitcase.

Before I can walk to the elevator, Tristan takes the handle, winks, causing flutters to rise in my stomach, and gestures for me to go ahead of him.

As I make my way, I realize it's going to be a long weekend sharing a room with this man.

It's going to be an even longer one than I imagined because now I'm in my hotel room, I'm staring at one lone bed and I groan.

# CHAPTER TWO

## Kaylee

I STARE AT the king-size bed in disbelief.

Behind me, Tristan stops short. "What's wrong?" he asks, stepping around me and following my gaze. "Oh. There's just one bed."

"I planned on reminding her but that woman with her crying kids interrupted me and I forgot." Sharing a room is something I can handle. Sharing a bed, however? Not so much, I think, and bite down on my lower lip. "This is a mistake. I'll call the front desk and get it sorted out."

I do, and the woman who checked me in confirms I booked a double with two queen beds. Relief fills me until she explains they're fully booked, as they told the older couple, and there are no other available rooms to switch. She apologizes profusely and I hang up, assuring her it's not her fault.

"We're stuck with this room, aren't we?" Tristan asks. He's moved to the bed, sitting on the edge and leaning back on his elbows, looking extremely relaxed and even more sexy than usual.

I know it's not intentional, but he's doing nothing to make this situation any easier. "What is up with this resort?" I ask, frustration lacing my tone. "First, they nearly ruined that other couple's anniversary, and now they've given me the wrong room."

"Did you also use a third-party booking site?" he asks.

I turn to find him smirking and I laugh, letting the stress go. "No, if I'd done that, we wouldn't even have this room." I fold my arms across my chest and look toward the window, where I see the sun has now fully set. Darkness cloaks the outdoors and we're safe inside. That's all I can ask for.

"We'll make do," I tell him.

He nods, easing up to a sitting position. "And if not for you, I'd have been stuck sleeping in my car. Sleeping on the couch is an upgrade."

"You really are an optimist," I say to him. A glance toward the sitting area and I see the couch in question is a loveseat. Way too small for a man as tall as Tristan. It's even a little small for me, but I'll fit better than he will. "There's no way you'll fit. I'll take the couch."

He's already shaking his head before I finish speaking. "No way. I'll sleep on the sofa, you take the bed."

I can't help but smirk. "An optimist *and* a gentleman? How did I get so lucky?" His eyes light up in amusement at my teasing, but I'm not letting him get his way. "I'm taking the couch," I insist.

He rubs his hand along the back of his neck, then shakes his head at me. "I had no idea you were so stubborn," he says, standing.

"I come by it naturally," I mutter.

"Well, if there's one thing my grandfather taught me, it's to put a woman's comfort and safety above my own. He'd roll over in his grave if I let you sleep on that tiny couch while I'm stretched out on a bed that was yours to begin with." He pulls up the handle on his suitcase, drags it to the sitting area, and plops it onto the couch, as if that settles things.

I'm about to argue further, enjoying this banter more than any disagreement I've had before, but my phone goes off. I grab it from my bag and see it's a text. "It's Ashley. She's reminding me the dinner starts in thirty minutes."

My cousin knows I get easily distracted and even on her wedding weekend, she takes time to remind me not to be late. With people I love, I don't take it personally, I'm grateful for them. With assholes who use my weaknesses against me? Another story entirely, I think, remembering Mark without any fondness.

"We have half an hour to meet everyone downstairs," I tell Tristan. "I'm looking forward to dinner. I've heard the restaurant has an amazing seafood menu." And I do enjoy lobster.

Tristan looks out the window, where the ocean is visible, the newly risen moon reflected on the surface. "I hope so. I'd love lobster tonight and since we're by the water, hopefully that's one of the selections."

I laugh. "I was just thinking that myself. Umm, I need to freshen up and change. Mind if I use the bathroom?" I tip my head toward the open door across the way.

"Be my guest. I can change out here."

I glance from him to the suitcase on the sofa and back again. "We'll pick up the conversation of who sleeps where when we get back. By the way, I intend to win." Not wanting to argue now, I spin on my heel and step over to my suitcase, but Tristan is there and lifts it onto the opened luggage stand.

"Thanks."

"No problem," he says.

I get my things together and stride into the bathroom where I touch up my lipstick and run my fingers through my long hair. I had my blonde highlights done at the salon yesterday, and I'm happy with the results. I may be dateless, but at least I look good.

I change into a hot pink sundress, turning to see the final look in the mirror. The neckline dips low enough to show off my cleavage in a tasteful way. Not enough to look tacky or get any tongues wagging at the wedding.

I just don't want to deal with the "Oh, poor Kaylee, her boyfriend dumped her before her cousin's wedding. No matter how many times I might tell them he's just sick—okay, I was going to pretend Cole was my boyfriend to avoid pitying glances—they'll assume the worst, like a breakup or being dumped the morning we were supposed to leave. That's the way it goes when your ex-boyfriend is attending the same wedding with the woman he started dating just two weeks after your relationship ended.

It doesn't matter that I'm perfectly happy with my situation and better off without Mark's emotional distance or critical comments. Never mind the fact that *I'm* the one who dumped *him*. All everyone is going to see is a thirty-year-old woman that still hasn't moved on. The truth doesn't matter. The optics do. That's why I invited my friend to be my date this weekend. It's just a shame he couldn't make it. All I can do is act like I don't mind being here alone.

I walk out of the bathroom to find Tristan has changed clothing from the dark jeans and collared short-sleeve shirt to a pair of black slacks and a white dress shirt that's unbuttoned at the collar. No matter what he wears, he draws me to him. Pathetic, but true. The scent of his cologne fills the room and ignites the desire I thought I'd banked earlier.

"Hi," I say so he knows I'm here.

He turns, sees me, and his sexy mouth lifts in a wide grin. "You look gorgeous," he tells me, and it's all I can do not to swoon.

I smile and give a little curtsey.

"Ready?" he asks.

I lift my shoes from the suitcase, slip into the pumps, and quickly put a few necessities into a small purse. "Now I am."

Together we head to the elevator and take it down to the first floor where the restaurant is located. All the information is on the couple's website and I've memorized most of what we need to know. I'm good at that, though not at getting to places on time. But tonight I managed.

When we step off the elevator, it's obvious the crowd has thinned. The rush of people arriving to check in is much smaller and we only have to dodge a single luggage cart as we make our way to the restaurant. There's a hostess stand just inside the entrance, and beyond her is a horseshoe-shaped bar area where I see several familiar faces there, but the bride and groom are yet to arrive.

The hostess turns to us. "Can I help you?"

"We're with the wedding party," Tristan tells her.

Her gaze runs over him and a small smile lifts her lips. Yes, he's impressive, I think to myself, hating how other women react to Tristan. Which is ridiculous.

He's not my date.

She nods. "You can join everyone inside," she says, gesturing toward the bar area.

We walk inside and look for Rainey and Lucas, but so far they aren't here. In the corner of the room, my mother is talking with my aunt Joanne, the mother of the bride, and Ashley's friend, Paige, another bridesmaid, is flirting with a blond-haired man. Her glassy eyes make her look like she's already had a little too much to drink, and I know she's one of my cousin's louder friends. I hope the alcohol doesn't make things worse.

"I'm going to grab a beer," Tristan says. "Can I get you anything?"

I shake my head. "No, thank you. I'll go talk to my mom." I tip my head toward where she's standing.

"Okay. I'll see you later." He strides over to the bar and leans in.

The pretty bartender's eyes light up when she sees him, and I sigh. None of your business, I tell myself, even as I wonder if he'll ask for her phone number.

I shake my head and spin around in the opposite direction.

"Kaylee!" I recognize his voice before I see his face, and my shoulders bunch up with tension.

I force a plastic smile and slowly pivot to face my ex, his arm draped around the shoulders of a woman with an hourglass figure and pouty lips. She runs an assessing gaze over me, and I straighten my shoulders. I understand her interest. After all, I'm the ex and she's bound to be curious.

"Mark," I say, in a deliberately neutral voice. "How have you been?"

"I'm great." He steps in close and briefly gives me a one-arm hug. It's not intimate but still more physical contact than I'm comfortable with, and I stiffen until he steps back. "Kaylee, this is my girlfriend, Shannon."

She meets my gaze and steps closer to him. I can't tell if she's worried about me or just staking her claim. Either way, I'm not jealous and she has nothing to worry about. I ended my relationship with Mark for good reason, but I still felt guilty because we'd been together for two years and I had feelings for him, even if they didn't run as deep as they should have. But he lost his mind when I broke up with him. For a man too emotionally stunted to say *I love you*, he was quick to anger and spit out cruel comments that stung. He pointed out all of my flaws and given how some of them were on point, he accomplished his goal of hurting me.

Forcing myself off that train of thought, I meet Shannon's gaze. "It's nice to meet you," I say honestly.

She blinks, a flicker of surprise in her gaze. Had she expected me to be catty and mean?

Mark takes her hand, intertwining their fingers and treating me to his smug smile. "Shannon might look familiar to you. She's a weatherwoman," he says with pride, as if her accomplishments are his.

"Congratulations," I say. "But I'm afraid I get my weather forecast from an app on my phone. I'll have to watch. What channel are you on?"

She tells me the station, and I store it in the back of my mind.

"I understand. Thank goodness enough people like the human touch that comes from a real meteorologist," Shannon says with pride she earned, followed by a glare at Mark.

My eyebrows pop up as I look at his clueless face. He called her a *weatherwoman*, suggesting she just points at cloud formations on a television screen and looks pretty. But she's a physical scientist and I'm impressed. My ex is a moron, something confirmed when he listed my flaws and informed me I'd have problems finding another man, as if I should stay with him for that reason alone. I stuck to my decision and informed him I'd have no trouble replacing him. And that's probably true, but I don't date for the sake of not being alone. I need to feel a spark, which hasn't happened since I dumped Mark.

"I'm impressed," I tell Shannon. "I promise to check out one of your broadcasts."

Her lips part in surprise. I have no doubt Mark told her I'd be a bitch. I merely look at her and smile. Though our breakup killed any remaining feelings I had for Mark, he wounded my pride and being here alone while he's shoving his girlfriend in my face is irritating. I just want to get away as cleanly and quickly as possible. Glancing around, I see my mother is talking to someone else. Aunt Joanne has too many responsibilities to talk to one person all evening.

"And what about you, Kaylee?" Mark asks, redirecting my focus to him again. "Where's your date?"

I take a deep breath and straighten my spine, determined not to let him bother me. I open my mouth to admit I'm here alone when I feel a warm body and an arm brushing against mine. I glance up to see Tristan beside me with a smile on his face.

He hands me a glass of wine and I notice a glint in his eye that I can't read.

I accept the drink I didn't ask for as he loops one arm around my waist, gripping my hip and pulling my body flush against his. Every inch of his sculpted form eases against my side and the temptation to melt into him is strong.

What the hell is he doing?

"Mark, it's good see you, man," Tristan says. "And to answer your question, I'm right here." Until this moment, I forgot they even knew each other. Since

Mark is the groom's best friend and Tristan is also in the wedding, of course they're either friends or acquaintances.

Mark frowns, his eyes darting back and forth between Tristan and me. "Excuse me?"

"You asked where Kaylee's date is," Tristan says, pausing to take a sip of his beer. "I'm right here. Right, honey?"

# CHAPTER THREE

## *Tristan*

IVE MINUTES AGO, I was at the bar, sipping from a glass of beer with a perfect foamy top and trying to avoid the bartender's roaming eye and blatant interest. She'd been giving me *the look* since I walked up to get my drink, but I'm not interested. As I looked around the room, my gaze zeroed in on Kaylee, watching her ex approach with his new girlfriend.

I don't know the details of Kaylee and Mark's breakup, but Rainey indicated it wasn't pretty. Even from a distance, I noticed her straighten her shoulders, her entire body stiff, the opposite of the relaxed, smiling woman I rode down the elevator with.

Mark's cocky smirk and Kaylee's discomfort told me all I needed to know.

She could use some backup.

I ordered a glass of red wine, tossed cash onto the bar without taking the napkin with the bartender's phone number scrawled across it in blue pen, and strode over to Kaylee. I heard Mark's question and I didn't stop to think. I slid in next to her, pulled her lush body against mine, and announced myself as her date.

"You?" Mark asks in disbelief. "You're kidding, right?"

Kaylee makes a noise that sounds like an indignant scoff. "Don't be rude, Mark. He told you he's my date. And he is." She looks up at me with something like adoration in her sparkling gaze, impressing me. I've thrown her a curveball and she's running with it.

Mark's eyes narrow and I can't hold back my grin.

"You guys … uh … you don't seem like a likely pairing," Mark finally says. "Kaylee's a relationship kind of woman."

I open my mouth to speak, but Kaylee jumps in first.

"Don't presume to speak for me, Mark." She eases the words by softening her voice, but I know she's annoyed.

Still, I get what Mark's saying. He thinks I'm a player, but I'm not. Sure, I do the casual sex thing. It's fun and easy, but I'm looking for a serious relationship. I just haven't found the right woman and usually realize pretty quickly whoever I'm with isn't the one, so I end things and don't look back.

Why dwell on the past when the person wasn't right for me to begin with? But the ease with which I move on has given me the reputation of a playboy.

I've never let anyone's opinion bother me. *I* know I don't use woman and discard them, so gossip doesn't matter.

I realize Mark is still staring and I need to step in. "I guess I'm just lucky Kaylee gave me a chance despite my reputation," I say to her ex.

I've never liked the man. He's Eric's best friend, so we've hung out a few times, and he comes across as too self-involved. All he ever talks about is himself. Though I have to admit, he's not doing that now. In fact, he's stewing in silence as he grinds his teeth together and glares at us in silence. His girlfriend, meanwhile, is shifting from foot to foot, obviously uncomfortable.

I sip my beer and keep my grip on Kaylee who's staring at me in shock. I absentmindedly rub my thumb along her hip, and she shudders. She's so sensitive and responsive, my cock grows heavy in my pants. A crowded restaurant isn't the best place to get an erection, but I doubt anyone will notice.

To help sell our relationship, I tuck a stray strand of blonde hair behind her ear and stare into her eyes, silently willing her to relax. For just a moment, everyone else in the restaurant fades away. Kaylee's breath escapes through her plump, parted lips. Only inches separate us and her pupils expand as she looks into my eyes. The air is thick with sexual tension, and I forget about pretending for the sake of Kaylee's ex. I forget about the reason we're even here. She's awakened a hunger inside me and I *need* a taste.

But just when I'm about to lean in and steal a kiss, Mark clears his throat. "There's no need for the two of you to be all over each other," he says, jaw tight.

Kaylee shifts away, and the interruption is like being doused with cold water. The rest of the world comes back into focus around us, and the fire that's burning through my veins cools. For now.

"Come on, Shannon. We're going to get a drink."

She stares at us, brow furrowed, eyes narrowed, and I wonder if he realizes how obvious his jealousy is.

He turns away and stalks toward the bar, not bothering to make sure Shannon is following.

"What the hell was that?" Kaylee asks, sounding more confused than angry. "What were you thinking declaring us a couple?"

I let out a chuckle. "Isn't it obvious? I just saved you from an awkward situation."

She shakes her head. "You know we're here for the next *three days*, right? If we don't keep up the ruse, it'll be way more embarrassing for me."

Something I'd never let happen.

I like Kaylee. We've known each other for a while, though we aren't close. But I've noticed her whenever she's at the club with Rainey. Not only is she pretty, she smiles often and, best of all, she's self-aware and unpretentious. Given her friendship with my best friend's fiancée, I've steered clear. We've never interacted one-on-one for a prolonged period of time. Never been this close before. Her hair smells like coconut, and I can feel the warmth of her skin through the thin fabric of her dress.

"Well?" she asks, and I realize my thoughts drifted.

At this point, I'm noticing too much about her, and I step back and take another sip of my beer. "Well, sweetheart. I guess that means I'm your boyfriend for the weekend."

Which won't be a hardship for me.

# CHAPTER FOUR

## *Kaylee*

T HERE'S A KNOT forming between my stiff shoulder blades, and I can't seem to stop bouncing my leg. Ever since Tristan pronounced us as a couple, I've been worried. Mark is watching our every move and my family is here. I'm going to have to lie to them and I hate the thought.

We've moved into the main room and are seated at a long table next to a window. I'm hyperaware of Tristan on my right. He's correct when he says he saved me from an awkward situation, and I appreciate he stepped in when he did, but I'm out of practice being casually intimate with a *real* boyfriend. Pretending to have that kind of relationship with Tristan, a man I'm so attracted to, feels impossible.

Beneath the table, he places a hand on my knee, stopping my leg from bouncing. At the feel of his palm on my bare skin, a shiver runs down my spine, and I whip my head in his direction so fast I feel dizzy.

"Relax," he whispers.

I look at him, stunned. Unlike me, he seems completely at ease, which he proves with a wink in my direction. "You seem a little on edge, sweetheart."

*Sweetheart.* That's what he called me earlier. The term of endearment slips so easily from his lips, and hearing it feels way too good and natural. Like this thing between us is real.

Like the moment we shared just before Mark stormed away. For a split second, I thought Tristan would kiss me. Even the memory of that heated interaction causes my stomach to swoop with hope and desire. My eyes flicker to his lips and when Tristan smirks, I'm sure my thoughts are imprinted on my forehead.

"I'm fine," I lie, and his smirk merely widens.

To add to tonight's stress, we are seated across the table from Mark and his date. I can *feel* his stare, sense that he's looking at me. Knowing he's probably trying to listen to our conversation, I decide to try out a cute nickname of my own on Tristan.

"… Babycakes?"

*Babycakes?* Where the hell did that come from?

Tristan laughs, and even though it's at my expense, the sound hits me right in the center of my chest. It's light and warm, and I *like* the way his eyes brighten and crinkle in the corners. Thanks to a silly interaction, I find myself relaxing as I smile in return. I'm not even embarrassed by my pitiful attempt at a cute nickname.

I'm glad I amused him.

"I love your romantic nicknames," he says, when he's gotten his laughter under control. Despite the fact that this isn't an intimate moment, I have the crazy urge to lean in and press a kiss to his lips. Which scares me because this is starting to feel like much more than a fake date.

"Swordfish?" a waiter asks, appearing at my side. I'm thankful for the distraction because I'm not sure how to handle the fluttering feeling in my chest.

"Yes, thank you," I say. Tristan's seafood pasta is placed in front of him, and it smells amazing.

"Still upset they didn't have lobster?" he asks.

I grin and shake my head. "I'm so hungry I'm not sure it matters what they put in front of me. Yours looks delicious."

"Would you like to try some?" Tristan doesn't wait for my response before placing one muscle and a clam on the edge of my own plate.

From across the table, I hear Mark's familiar sound of disapproval. I didn't realize just how judgmental he could be until I ended things. Now, that tsking noise he makes with his tongue against the roof of his mouth brings back memories of him criticizing me for every small mistake I made during our two years together. I wish I'd picked up on it and done something sooner rather than put up with his constant critiques.

I glance over, and there's a dark look on his face that's also familiar. His disdain along with his attention is completely focused on me.

"Problem?" I ask, my own irritation sounding louder than I'd meant it to be.

"Not at all," he says, but that narrowing of his gaze says differently. "I just think it's funny how some things never change."

"What does *that* mean?" Even as I ask, I wonder why I'm engaging with him.

He shrugs. "Just that you never know what you want. You're always changing your mind after you've already ordered."

I blink. *Seriously?*

"And it's not just about food. You're fickle," he mutters.

I hear a snicker and feel the stares of the others at the table. I flush with embarrassment, but I won't let him belittle me.

Beside me, Tristan stiffens, but I place my hand on his muscular thigh and squeeze, letting him know I've got this.

I narrow my gaze at Mark. "Are you saying I have second thoughts about breaking up with you? Because I can assure you, I don't." I casually pat my lips with my napkin and treat him to a sickly-sweet smile.

Mark's face grows red, and I regret my words. Not because they aren't true, but because I don't want to make a scene. Ashley, sitting nearby, leans over and whispers something to him that ends in a heated conversation before her fiancé shuts it down.

"I'm sorry," I mouth to my cousin, who shakes her head. I know she means it's not my fault, but I feel bad.

"Look at you, putting a man in his place without breaking a sweat," Tristan says quietly, and I slap his arm.

"Don't encourage me. That could've turned into something ugly." And I'd never forgive myself if I ruined any part of Ashley's weekend.

Still, I can't deny I'm also getting a little satisfaction from Mark's obvious discomfort. After the way he tore me down during the breakup, payback feels good. And I have Tristan to thank for putting me in the position to do so. If he wasn't pretending to be my date, if I were here alone, I might not have the opportunity to put Mark in his place.

I feel someone behind me and tip my head to see my mother is standing. I pivot so I can face her.

"Kaylee, who is this man?" my mother asks, eyeing Tristan with an assessing gaze. I'm not sure how much of our conversation she's overheard, but based on her pinched lips, it was enough.

"I'm Tristan Hayes," he says, rising and holding out his hand for her to shake.

When she takes it, he flips her hand over and kisses the back in a move that makes me roll my eyes.

He's such a flirt.

"The best man?" she asks, and I'm not surprised she recognizes the name since she helped handle the wedding programs.

"Yes, ma'am," he says with the most polite wording.

My mother smiles, her eyes shifting to me. "Oh, I like him, Kay."

*Me too, Mom. Me too.* I merely smile.

"So, is this your boyfriend?" she asks.

The only thing more humiliating than being here alone would be getting caught lying about having a date, but I wouldn't lie to my mom for my own sake. If I don't keep up the pretense, however, I'll humiliate myself and Tristan. And he's gone out of his way to make this weekend easier for me.

"We're new," I say, not exactly answering her question, therefore not completely lying, either.

Tristan leans back, placing an arm along the back of my chair. "We've known each other through mutual friends, but we've just started getting to know one another better." His words, like mine, aren't exactly a lie, either.

For the next five minutes, my mom peppers Tristan with questions about himself. His hobbies, his job, his favorite football team. None of it gets very deep, and he's a good sport, answering her questions and making small talk like it's his job.

Finally, my dad comes over to get her for dinner, shakes Tristan's hand, and leads her away.

Then, we eat, and the conversation around us flows easily. I ignore Mark and Shannon across the table, and it doesn't take long before I'm relaxed and enjoying myself. Tristan plays the doting boyfriend so effortlessly I find myself falling into my own role of smitten girlfriend. The chemistry between us grows stronger with each flirty interaction, to the point where it's overwhelming. I can't seem to stop thinking about that potential kiss from earlier and hope there's a chance for a real one later.

But my fantasy doesn't stop there. Desire settles low in my belly, and my thighs clench as I imagine where that kiss might lead. Would the spark between us rage out of control? Would he grind against me? Touch my body with a senseless hunger that turns me into a puddle of satisfied goo? Or is he a slow lover who takes his time to savor each moment?

Gah! I can't do this. My body is tingling and sensitive and I reach for my glass of water, nearly knocking it over in the process.

"Are you okay?" Tristan asks.

I nod and take a long sip of cold water, hoping it helps quell the need my thoughts inspired.

Finally, our meal ends, and Ashley and Eric stand. Where my cousin is petite and thin with platinum blonde hair, light blue eyes, and fair skin, Eric is tall and solidly built with black hair and dark brown eyes. Despite those differences, they *fit* together in a way I've always been envious of. Not in a mean or negative way, but in a lesson learned type of way.

In fact, their engagement is part of the reason I ended things with Mark last year. Seeing how excited they were to start their lives together shined a harsh light on the fact that there were issues. Mark was utterly unwilling to commit, not even to live together after a two-year relationship. I'd always known he had issues, but I thought over time he'd come around.

It had taken the ease and softness of Ash and Eric's relationship to show me I was too willing to settle. I wasn't taking into account the red flags with Mark. His criticism. His temper, not that he'd ever taken his anger out on me physically. But I didn't want to walk on eggshells any longer, either. Not to mention Mark is a workaholic. He hated getting emotional and wouldn't share his feelings. For a variety of reasons, he wasn't the man I wanted to settle down with.

As Ashley gives a speech thanking all of us for

traveling here for the wedding, I barely register what she's saying. I'm watching the way Eric looks at her; it's like she hung the moon. *I want that.* I want a man that not only feels deeply about me but isn't afraid to show it to everyone. I want a love like the one that Ashley and Eric share.

"To show our appreciation to the entire wedding party, Eric and I got gifts for our bridesmaids and groomsmen," Ashley says.

Gifts are passed out, watches for the men and necklaces for the women. The necklace is a delicate silver chain with a pink, heart-shaped pendant. It's simple but beautiful. I lift it out of the box, and Tristan reaches for it.

"Let me," he says, opening the necklace with surprisingly deft fingers.

I only hesitate for a moment before turning and lifting my hair off my neck. Tristan drapes the jewelry around me, and I feel his fingertips brush against my skin as he clasps the necklace. My pulse races and goosebumps break out over my arms. The magnetic pull I feel toward him is a hum beneath my skin.

"So, Tristan," Mark says as I turn back around in my chair. His voice is slurred and I wonder how many drinks he's had. "What happened between you and that really hot model you dated earlier this year?"

My stomach drops. Annika was a model. Gorgeous

in an ice-cold kind of way. If I were taking stock of the differences between us … I cut off those thoughts. Tristan isn't my real boyfriend, and I'm good with who I am.

I glance at Tristan, who smiles at Mark as if he's not getting to him, but there's a slight tic of a muscle in his jaw that tells me he's not happy with the turn in conversation.

"You mean Annika? We didn't date for long."

Mark shakes his head and lets out a low whistle. "Man, you must have been crazy to let a knockout like her go."

At his words, conversation dies out around the table. It seems that everyone's attention is on Mark and Tristan and, by extension, me. It's awkward and uncomfortable.

Tristan relaxes, his eyes locked on Mark, and leans forward, elbows on the table. "I'm curious why you care. After all, you're here with your girlfriend. What does my social life have to do with you?"

At that, Mark's face becomes flushed and he turns to Shannon, who is already glaring at him.

"He makes a damn good point, Mark," she snaps, tossing her cloth napkin onto the table as she surges to her feet. With grace that must be difficult in this situation, she walks away from the table with her head held high, leaving Mark to fumble through getting to his feet and stumbling after her with an apology on his lips.

It's petty, but I can't help the glee surging through me because Mark had been trying to embarrass me by bringing up Tristan's ex-girlfriend, but he only embarrassed himself instead.

Conversation resumes around the table, and I lean in close to Tristan, whispering in his ear, "You're the best fake boyfriend ever."

He chuckles but when he turns to me, his eyes dark and serious, my entire body is suddenly on fire. "You handle yourself well, Kaylee. I like how you don't take his shit. I'm just backup for you."

Warmth and pride slide through me at his words. Knowing Tristan admires how I handled Mark leaves me with a glow, inside and out.

# CHAPTER FIVE

## *Tristan*

I WAKE UP slowly and it takes a moment to get my bearings. Sunlight warms my face, telling me I'm not home because my heavy blackout curtains keep out all light. My second clue comes when I register a weight on my body. There's a person draped over my chest. I never let a woman stay over because, again … I refuse to give out the wrong signal. I can leave easily from their place, whereas I'd be stuck with a visitor at my apartment.

As the fog clears, yesterday comes back to me. The hotel, sharing a room and a bed …

Kaylee.

I open my eyes, blinking a few times to adjust to the natural light peeking in through the hotel room window, where we left the curtains open last night. When my vision has adjusted, I look down to see Kaylee's face. Her eyes are closed and her mouth is slightly open as she takes deep breaths in and out. She's still asleep, utterly relaxed against me, no clue that she didn't stay on her own side of the bed as she insisted we would last night. I smirk as I imagine what her reaction would be when she realizes *she* moved on top of me.

After dinner, we returned to the hotel room, both too tired to argue about who would sleep on the couch. We decided, like two responsible adults with self-control, that we could handle sharing the large bed and staying on our own sides.

Never mind the fact that my cock was achingly hard as I tried to fall asleep in the dark, way too aware of her body across from mine. I'd gotten a brief glance of her in her pajamas, a pair of white cotton shorts and a hot pink tank top, and the idea of ripping those clothes off of her body made it hard to get my erection under control. I lay up long after I heard her breathing slow and sleep found her.

When I finally succumbed to sleep, she was still on her side of the bed, so I'm not sure when she rolled on top of me, but I have no complaints. Since she's still out cold, I allow myself a small indulgence, running my hands through her blonde hair. It's just as soft as it looks, and my mind conjures up the image of those strands wrapped around my fist while I fuck her from behind.

With that picture in my mind, I roll her over and wait to see if she wakes. A little snore escapes and I learn she's a very deep sleeper. Grinning, I slip out of bed, making sure not to wake her up. I head to the bathroom, turn on the shower, and step under the stream of water before it's fully warmed up, hoping the shock of the cold water will help cool my blood.

It doesn't work. My mind lingers on the feel of her body pressed against mine, the chemistry that burned so brightly between us last night, and the desire that has turned my cock into a steel rod. I attempt to ignore it while I wash my hair and clean my body, but my erection doesn't go away.

I can't walk around like this all day. I need to try to take the edge off. Bracing one hand on the tile wall, I lean forward so the water hits my back between my shoulder blades. Eyes closed, I grip my cock with my free hand and stroke it from base to tip. A hiss escapes me.

I let my imagination run wild, picturing Kaylee here with me, skin slick and flushed as she sinks to her knees. Her lips part and she locks those blue eyes on my face as she grasps my dick and guides it to her mouth.

Biting my lip, I hold back a moan and move my hand faster, squeezing just enough to heighten my pleasure as I imagine that pouty mouth taking me in, her cheeks hollowed and nipples peaked. I wonder if I could hold off long enough to take her against the wall or if she'd suck me until I exploded, swallowing every last drop.

That mental image is enough to drive me over the edge, and my hips jerk forward as my release hits the tile wall. I stroke myself through my climax, letting out a muffled grunt but holding back the urge to make more noise. I don't want Kaylee to hear me. It'd be too damn tempting to pull her into the shower and make my fantasy come to life.

I need to stay on schedule. I'm supposed to meet the guys for breakfast, so I can't make a move on Kaylee now, but later, if she's willing, I don't think I'll be able to hold myself back.

I grabbed clothes before I came into the bathroom, so I get dressed and go through the rest of my morning routine before I step back into the room where Kaylee is still sleeping. She's spread eagle on the bed, taking up as much room as possible, and I grin, a foreign feeling washing over me. Like a surge of affection for the woman in the bed we shared.

Smiling to myself, I tuck my key card for the room into my pocket and head to the coffee shop in the lobby of the hotel. It's only open in the mornings, and they have a selection of pastries. The guys decided we'd do casual. No need to sit in the restaurant for regular service. I buy a mocha and a blueberry muffin and head to a table on the terrace, where Lucas is the only one already here.

I reach the table and have no time to put my food down when he's in my personal space. "What the hell is going on with you and Kaylee?" he asks.

Last night, he'd been sitting a ways down the table, so I assume he missed a lot of what happened. Though we hadn't had a chance to talk afterward, there's no doubt he'd heard all about it. Especially about the part where Mark lost his shit because Kaylee and I were a couple. Most people at the wedding might believe the story we told last night—that we recently started dating—but Lucas is my closest friend and business partner. *And* he happens to be engaged to Kaylee's friend and business partner. If we were really dating, no matter how recent it might be, Lucas and Rainey would know about it.

"Didn't you hear? She's my girl," I say with a cheeky grin as I take the wrapper off my muffin.

"Get serious. What's going on?"

"Sit down, relax, and I'll tell you."

He mutters something I don't hear and takes a seat.

Between sips of coffee, I tell him the truth. He's not a big fan of Mark either, and I can tell he approves of me stepping in to help her deal with him by pretending to be her date. Then, I fill him in on the room mix-up and how we ended up sharing one.

His eyes grow wide. "One bed? Does that mean

you *are* sleeping together?"

"In the literal sense, yes. But we're each staying on our own side of the bed." That's not necessarily true, but in this case, I think intent is more relevant than execution. "As for sex … Well, nothing has happened on that front. Yet."

"Yet? Wow." Lucas leans back in his seat, running a hand through his dark hair. "You never mentioned having a thing for Kaylee before."

I understand his point. "I didn't. I mean, she's hot, but I didn't really think of her like that." What I don't tell him is that something shifted between us last night.

There are a lot of beautiful women in the world, and I've dated plenty of them, but there's always been something missing. I want more than just empty sex or frivolous fun. I want to feel a connection. It's the main reason I've had so many short-term relationships. I don't want to settle. I'm looking for something deeper than surface level and last night, the chemistry we shared felt like it ran deeper than the physical attraction between us. I felt it even if I can't explain why.

There's potential with Kaylee, and the idea of exploring that is exciting. She could be the one I've been looking for, and I almost missed it because I was pursuing the wrong women. "You know, Kaylee is different from any woman I've dated in the past." I don't want Lucas to feel like I'm using her in any way.

Just then, a chair is pulled out beside me. I glance up as Eric slides into the seat. Mark ends up across from me, next to Lucas.

"Morning, boys," Eric says with a grin.

"You're in a good mood," I comment, taking a big bite of my muffin. Not that I blame him.

"Of course I am. I'm getting married tomorrow."

Mark rolls his eyes, but I'm the only one that seems to notice and he covers it with a sip of his coffee.

"Good for you," Lucas says. "I'm looking forward to tying the knot too. I've wanted to lock Rainey down for a while, but she's planning a big wedding. And what she wants? She gets."

"That's what happens with a family name like Dare," Eric says. "Big money means a big party."

Lucas laughs. "It's not about that for me or for Rainey. Her mother is over the moon her only daughter is getting married. I'm letting them do whatever they want. I'll just be glad when I can call Rainey my wife."

"You guys are so whipped," Mark says, but everyone ignores him.

He's surly this morning, and he's actively avoiding my gaze. He doesn't say much as we eat breakfast and talk about the schedule for the next couple of days. I wonder if Eric said something to him after he made an ass of himself last night and now he's on a tight leash.

We linger in the coffee shop for a while, until it's time to meet the girls at the dock for a wedding party boat and snorkeling expedition planned by Ashley. Despite living in Miami and spending a ton of time at the beach, I've never been snorkeling before. Personally, I'd rather be surfing, but swimming around in the ocean sounds more appealing than it did before yesterday because it means I'll be with Kaylee.

When we get to the dock, the women are waiting in a group. Ashley and Kaylee are talking, and I allow my eyes to roam over her from head to toe, starting with the oversized sunglasses on her face and working my way down. She's wearing a dress again. This time, it's white with an eyelet pattern. It hugs her chest before flowing to just above her knees. It's not particularly revealing, but she looks stunning. I focus my gaze on her long legs, internally cursing when the thought of having them wrapped around me makes my dick jerk back to life.

*So much for taking the edge off.* I have a feeling taking care of myself isn't going to give me the satisfaction I truly need.

Mark's girlfriend is among the women, and she comes to his side but it's obvious the awkward tension between them remains. She's stiff and he has that bored look that doesn't bode well for her.

I focus on Kaylee as she greets me with a smile. "Hi, there. How did you sleep last night? Sharing a bed wasn't too bad, right?" she asks.

I think about waking up with the scent of her coconut shampoo in my nose and her warm skin against mine. Clearly she has no recollection of draping herself over me. "No," I say, my lips curving in a grin. "Not bad at all."

"Time to load up!" someone yells out. We board the boat that's just big enough to fit our party of nine.

There are two bench seats, and I end up sitting between Eric and Kaylee who tilts her head back with a smile, as if she's trying to soak up the bright sunshine. When the boat starts moving, gliding over the waves, her hair whips wildly around, and I laugh when it hits me in the face.

It doesn't take long before we reach the reef the owner of the boat says is ideal for snorkeling.

Everyone stands.

Kaylee wastes no time pulling her dress over her head, and my mouth goes dry at the sight of her in a red bikini with miles of skin on display. Little triangles cover her breasts and my fingers itch with the urge to touch her beneath the barely-there material. Before I can talk to her, she moves toward the back of the boat and accepts a snorkel from a man in a Hawaiian shirt handing them out. I strip off my own shirt and kick off my shoes, leaving me in my swim trunks.

Keeping up with Kaylee is a challenge. I turn and she's already in the water. Finally, I join her and make my way over. "Hey!"

"Hi. Isn't this glorious?" We're treading and she tips her head back, hair in the water, as she closes her eyes and soaks up the sun on her face.

"This thing doesn't look very long," I say, holding up the snorkel. Everyone else is spreading out, already face down in the water, and I know I'm stalling.

Kaylee snickers. "The guy handing them out told me it's fifteen inches. Just stay near the surface. I don't want to have to give you CPR if you inhale a bunch of saltwater."

I can't help but grin. "What do I have to do to get a different kind of mouth-to-mouth?" I ask her.

Kaylee laughs as she splashes me. "Come on. Let's look at some fish." I note she ignored the question and realize I'm going to have to be less subtle.

Snorkeling turns out to be more fun than I expected. It takes a little while to get used to breathing through the tube, but I'm quickly distracted as I look around under the water. Sunlight pierces the surface in dancing patterns, and the world is made up of shades of blue. The coral reef is fascinating, with stony structures and purple vegetation. There are branching parts that remind me of deer antlers growing so high I can almost touch them.

I feel a tap on my arm and I look over at Kaylee. She's pointing out a school of neon blue fish passing directly in front of us, and even with her snorkel gear, I can sense her excitement.

*Adorable.*

We spend the next hour swimming around the reef together, pointing out fish and other sea creatures. I spot a grouper hiding in a crevice, and Kaylee gestures to a barracuda in the distance, its silver body still in the water as it waits for prey. The smaller fish come in every color imaginable, and it's easy to get swept up in the beauty of the ocean. Kaylee and I are hovering observers, not a part of the world below but appreciating it anyway.

When we surface, we tread water and talk about what we've seen, sharing light conversation and casual touches that arouse my desire. We've floated closer to each other and suddenly I realize only inches separate my bare chest and her barely covered one.

Her tongue darts out and she licks her lips. I bite back a groan but tread even closer, grasping her hips in my hands. It's been an amazing day, one I never anticipated. Her nipples rub against me, hard beneath the fabric of her bikini. Our gazes meet as she exhales, and I feel the warmth of her breath against my cheek. Unable to stop myself, I slide my hand along her jaw, tilting her head back, my intention clear.

Just as I'm about to brush my lips against hers, a voice rings out over the water. "Okay, folks," the owner of the boat calls out. "Time to head back."

I release a frustrated groan as Kaylee puts space between us, her cheeks a pretty pink. We lock eyes and grin, aware of what almost happened and clearly in agreement that we wanted it to.

I'm getting tired of interruptions when I'm about to give in to temptation. One way or another, I'm going to get my mouth on Kaylee Martin this weekend. I'm ready to turn this spark between us into an inferno.

# CHAPTER SIX

## *Kaylee*

WHEN THE BOAT arrives back at the dock, it's lunchtime. The group makes a decision to grab tacos at a concession stand on the beach. It's not far from the resort, and there's a volleyball net nearby. We all get fish tacos, a fitting choice for where we are, and we eat them while lounging in the sand. Tristan stays close to me, and I don't say anything, but I like it.

I just wish we hadn't been interrupted before kissing in the water. He was *so* close. Then again, maybe it's for the best. My desire for Tristan is strong, but that doesn't mean he's right for me. He's not the type to get serious with a woman, and I *only* do serious in my relationships. That's why Mark was surprised to see us together. He knows I'm not the casual type, and he's heard of Tristan's reputation as a player. There's a little voice in my head telling me to enjoy the weekend with him and I'm tempted to do just that, no matter where it takes me. Tristan just might be worth a little heartache when the wedding weekend is over.

After lunch, the men decide to join a few others on

the beach in a volleyball game. Ashley excuses herself to make a phone call, and I see Shannon heading back to the resort. Mark and his girlfriend have been subdued all day, and despite me not being directly at fault—I didn't start the arguments, and Mark was the one acting like an ass—I feel bad. I'm not the type to come between a couple, but Mark is going to have to get his act together or lose his current girlfriend.

I stay sitting in the sand as the guys start a game. I need to keep my sunglasses on to shield my eyes and wearing them lets me ogle Tristan in private. I bite my bottom lip as my gaze trails over his six-pack abs and down to the V-shape at his hips. Of course, he's still wearing his swim trunks, so there's nothing to see, but I *felt* him when we were about to kiss in the water, the bulge brushing against my stomach, large and unbelievably tempting.

Someone spikes the volleyball over the net, and I watch as Tristan dives forward, bumping it up with his forearms just before it hits the ground. He ends up with a face full of sand, but Lucas is able to send the ball back over the net. The other team didn't expect the save, so they aren't prepared, and they miss the ball.

I cheer for Tristan, even if the game is for fun and no one is keeping score.

"Hello, there." Rainey joins me, a margarita in each hand.

I take one from her and she plops down at my side, letting out an encouraging whoop as Lucas serves the ball over the net. "Go Lucas!" she calls out.

Next Tristan slams the ball down and I'm the one cheering.

"You're staring," Rainey says, nudging me with her shoulder.

I smirk and point to my sunglasses. "You can't know that."

"No, but you're putting out some unmistakable *I'm hot for Tristan* energy."

I can't help but laugh. "Come on, Rainey. I told you this morning in confidence, this thing between Tristan and me isn't real." I cornered her before we came down to the dock.

After hearing me tell my mom that Tristan was my boyfriend last night, Rainey had some serious questions. She's my best friend in the world, and the reason I even know Tristan, so I didn't want her in the dark. She's also the only person who knows about my crush on the guy.

My eyes drift to him again. Sweat now glistens on his skin, and my pussy clenches with need.

Who am I kidding? Before, I was thinking I was beyond tempted to take things further with Tristan, and now I'm sure. Despite the fact that I don't do casual relationships. I want time with Tristan badly enough that I'm willing to break my own rule and spend this weekend in his—our—bed. Based on the way he looked at me in the water earlier, like he wanted to devour me, I don't think I'll have any problem getting him to agree.

"You know, it's okay to like him for real," Rainey says in her soft, best friend voice.

I pull my gaze away from Tristan to find her watching me while she sips her margarita through a straw. She knows me too well.

"He's just helping me out and I appreciate him for that." I'm not sure why I don't want to be honest with her about my growing feelings for Tristan. I just know I'm already dealing with the feelings I'll have to face when the weekend is over. I may be going into this with my eyes wide open but I know it's going to hurt when it's over.

And I don't want Rainey, and, by extension Lucas, feeling torn or in the middle.

"Whatever you say. Just know I'm here if you want to hash things out in your head."

I smile at my friend. She knows me well enough to see right through me, but she also understands that I don't want to talk about it, so she'll let it go.

We spend the rest of the volleyball game checking out our men while sipping our drinks and shouting out words of praise and booing the other team.

When the game is over, Tristan accepts a bottle of water from one of the guys they played with, and I watch as he pours it over his head, shaking his hair out like he's in a shampoo commercial. Or like he's trying to kick my libido into high gear. If that's the case, he's succeeded.

Using the shirt he hasn't worn since we were on the boat, he wipes his face and strolls over to me with an easy smile on his face.

I tilt my head back as I look up at him. He holds out his hand. "Want to go for a walk, sweetheart?"

Rainey is the only one around when he speaks. Does he know I told her the truth? Or does he think she's in the dark? Is he calling me sweetheart for her benefit or does he mean it? At what point does this pretend game cross the line between faking it and having real feelings? For me, that's an easy answer. For Tristan? I'm not sure anything is real.

Yet I'm helpless to ignore my feelings.

"Sure," I say, putting my hand in his and letting him pull me to my feet. I hand my empty margarita cup to Rainey, who gives me a sly smile.

"Have fun," she chirps.

Giving her a goodbye wave, I fall into step beside Tristan and we head toward the water. When we reach the place where the waves stop, I slip off my flip-flops and carry them in one hand, enjoying the way the gooey sensation feels between my toes. Every time the water rises, it runs over my feet.

As we walk in silence, our arms brush against each other's and I'm happy, enjoying the easy silence but, as usual, I'm tempted to speak. "You're one hell of a volleyball player," I tell him.

He grins. "I enjoy the game, and I admit I have a competitive streak."

"Were you keeping score despite it being just for fun?" I ask.

"Maybe." He looks out over the ocean, and the wind tousles his dark hair, giving me more to admire. "Let's just say my team won."

I chuckle. "I get it. I've never been a big fan of the whole *participation trophy* thing they do in sports now. I've always thought that a win should be earned."

He nods. "Agreed. Tell me more about you, Kaylee."

I shrug, unsure of what to say. "What do you want to know?"

He thinks for a moment, then asks, "How do you spend a typical day off?"

"Hmm." I consider how to answer. I like that he's thinking outside the box. "Well, I'd start off by sleeping in. There's no better way to start your day than to wake up feeling well-rested. Then, I'd make myself French toast for breakfast. I'd want to spend the first half of my day doing something creative. Painting or scrapbooking or something like that. One time, I even took a basket-weaving class. It was surprisingly fun."

He smiles as if he's enjoying my answer. "I bet you're the type to give people handmade Christmas gifts, aren't you?"

"Of course. Those are the best kind. Don't you think?" I love creating things, giving personal gifts.

"Yes, actually, I do. Now, go on. You sleep in and do something creative. Then, what?"

I'm quiet for a moment, and Tristan gives me time to think. We've walked farther down the beach, our pace unhurried. We have time until the rehearsal dinner this evening, so there's no rush.

"After getting creative, I'd probably want some downtime. I love to read. Lately, my favorite thing to read is romantasy."

"Romantasy? What's that?" he asks, genuinely interested.

I stare at the water beyond me. "It's a romance set in a fantasy world. One with magic or dragons or fae. Sometimes the main characters start as enemies but become lovers. Or they're fated mates. That's my favorite trope," I muse out loud.

"Fated mates?" he asks.

I glance at him as he scrunches his nose up in curiosity.

"That means they're meant to be together?"

I nod. "Yep. Destiny. Isn't that romantic?"

He stops and I pause with him. "Actually, I prefer the idea of choosing the right person for you, someone you're so crazy about that you don't need fate to make the decision for you."

I nudge his arm. "Look at you. A closet romantic. Who knew?"

He meets my gaze and holds it, making me grateful for the sunglasses to hide whatever emotions he would otherwise find there. "Yeah, who knew?" he asks in a gruff voice.

I force an easy laugh, though my heart feels stuck in my throat.

Tristan glances back at the resort and sees how far we've walked. Without discussion, we turn and head back toward the hotel, in sync in a way that feels natural and good.

"Okay, so what's next on your day off? Dinner?" he asks.

I'm surprised he remembers our earlier conversation. I give the question some thought. "Sushi for dinner. Specifically from On a Roll. It's my favorite meal ever. Then, after dinner, I'd want to go out, maybe to Midnight."

He turns and looks at me. "You're not just saying that to suck up to me, are you?"

I shake my head. "Now, why would I do that?" I'm teasing him, and he knows it.

"Because you like me," he answers with an easy lift of his shoulders.

"So cocky," I mutter. "Now, you tell me something about *you*. Do you have a big family?" I ask.

"No, but I wish I did. I was raised by my grandparents because they were the only family I had left. My mom died giving birth to me, and my dad took off a few months later. I guess he just couldn't deal with being a single parent. He dropped me at my grandparents' house, my mom's parents. Then he took off. They were kind of stuck with me, I guess."

"Are you close with them?" I'm so curious about everything I can get from him.

He shakes his head. "They're both gone now. My grandfather died five years ago in a car accident, and my grandmother went just a few months later. Her heart gave out. A part of me thinks she just didn't want to live without him."

I reach for his hand and squeeze his fingers. "I'm so sorry. That's really awful."

We hold hands and swing arms as we walk. "I'm not going to lie. It was rough. But to answer your question, yes, we were close. I never really felt like I missed out on having parents because they stepped right in the role. I never felt like I was a burden they had to take on or that they resented me for their unexpected change in life."

"They sound like good people," I murmur, glancing up at him.

Tristan's smile is sad. "They were, and I miss them. In fact, I think that's part of the reason I gave that older couple my room. They reminded me of my grandparents."

We're still holding hands, not swinging, as we walk, and it feels right. "You know, my grandparents were a big part of my life too. They lived in New York, and I used to visit them every summer for about two weeks. They were always so happy to see me, and they made sure it was a fun experience for me."

"Oh yeah? Tell me." I feel the weight of his stare, the depth of his interest, and it warms me more than the sun.

"Well, one of my favorite memories is when my grandpa took me to see *The Lion King* on Broadway. I was probably around ten, and I *loved* the movie, so I couldn't wait to see the play. My grandpa was an old-school, flannel-wearing carpenter that had no time for the arts. But he sat right beside me for the whole show. He even sang along to a few of the songs, which surprised me, until he explained that he learned them for me. So that *I'd* have the best time possible." I smile at the memory, one I keep tucked away in my heart.

"They sound like amazing people," Tristan says.

"So do yours."

I was so lost in both the memory and talking to Tristan I barely noticed how close we'd gotten to the resort until he pulls on my hand until I stop. From the corner of my eye, I see people from the wedding party on the beach. Ashley and Rainey are laying out, working on their tans, while their significant others surf. Ashley's other bridesmaid, Paige, is flirting with a group of guys sitting under an umbrella. I don't see Mark and Shannon anywhere, but I'm not concerned about where they are.

In fact, as Tristan steps close to me, my mind blanks of everything but him. The anticipation is too much, and as I tilt my head back, my lips part, and I know this is it. We both want the kiss, and I'm not leaving this beach without knowing the feel of his mouth against mine.

"Kaylee," he says, running his fingers up my arms to my shoulders and then burying his hands in my hair. "I need to taste you. I'm dying to find out how good we are."

He doesn't ask for permission, but I know that's what he's looking for. I place my hands on his chest, my palms flat on his broad pecs. His sun-kissed skin is warm and smooth, and I want him. Everything about him.

"Yes," I breathe. "Tristan, yes."

With the yearning I see in his eyes, I expect it to be rough, a man taking what he wants so badly he loses control. But Tristan moves with slow intention. His mouth gently brushes over mine, the contact barely there, but he's still able to steal my breath. He teases me, nipping at my bottom lip, and I gasp, giving him the opening he needs to deepen the kiss.

His tongue slips inside, and I melt into him, a soft moan escaping, and he swallows the sound. My mouth moves against his and my heart pounds in my chest and as I press against him, it's his heart racing with an excitement that matches my own.

I've never ached like this, and all I can think about is getting him alone. I want *more* from this man. His grip tightens on my hair for a moment before he suddenly releases his hold. Then, he breaks the kiss but keeps me close, his forehead pressed against mine. "That was just the beginning, sweetheart. But now, we have to get ready for the rehearsal dinner."

*Damn it.* Another event before I finally get him to myself.

Tonight, I have no intention of staying on my side of the bed.

None at all.

# CHAPTER SEVEN

## *Kaylee*

LATER THAT NIGHT is the wedding rehearsal. We all have dinner in the resort's restaurant once again. This time, Mark is seated at the other end of the table, and I'm sure that was done intentionally and I'm grateful. I don't want more drama from the man, especially since tonight and tomorrow should only be about Ashley and Eric. They're important to me and the whole reason we're here. I don't want friction between me and my ex to ruin their special day. Tristan is seated beside me again. Any uncertainty or awkwardness I felt yesterday faded over the course of the day, and we chat easily with each other and the people around us.

After dinner, we head back to the beach. The sun has fully set, but the back of the resort has lights that illuminate its private stretch of beach, where the ceremony will take place tomorrow. White folding chairs are already set up in the sand along with an archway for the bride and groom. Aunt Joanne takes charge, going over how everything will proceed tomorrow. They plan a short and simple ceremony, with about fifty guests and an acoustic guitar player singing "Perfect" by Ed Sheeran, Ashley and Eric's song.

When Aunt Joanne directs the bridesmaids and groomsmen to stand together, Rainey and Lucas are together and Tristan is with Paige. As the maid of honor, I'm stuck walking beside Mark, something that never occurred to me. Ashley mouths, *I'm sorry*, to me and I shake my head. I can handle this for my cousin. At first, it really doesn't bother me. I'm truly over the man, and walking twenty feet at his side shouldn't be a big deal.

We stand beside each other, watching the other members of the wedding party walk together first.

"I'm worried about you, Kay-Kay," Mark says, using a nickname he gave me when we were together. Maybe he's trying to trigger sweet nostalgia, but he must be forgetting that I never liked that stupid, childish nickname.

"What are you talking about?" I ask, my eyes shifting to the movement ahead of us.

Tristan and Paige are walking toward the arch while Eric's mother clocks their timing. She and my aunt Joanne have decided they want to time the progression down the makeshift aisle so that the song being performed will end just as Ashley reaches the arch. It's a little intense for a laid-back beach wedding, but we're all just going with it. Before I went into the corporate event planning business, I interned for a wedding planner and I'm well aware it's a good idea to do whatever the mother of the bride or groom want, within reason, that is.

"I'm concerned about you dating Tristan," Mark says, pulling my attention back to him. "I don't think it's a good match. He's going to hurt you."

I narrow my eyes at him. "Tristan and I are none of your business. Now, be quiet and focus on the rehearsal," I mutter.

Tristan and Paige have reached the arch, so Rainey and Lucas begin their walk.

"I didn't want to tell you this," Mark says, his tone of voice contrary to his words. He's enjoying this conversation too much. "But I think you should know that I heard Tristan talking to Lucas this morning. He said you're different from his usual type, you know, all those models he's gone out with in the past. If he's already realized that, how long do you think he's going to stick around?"

I do my best not to throttle him, grinding my teeth to keep quiet. I know he's trying to hurt me, but I also know the truth. Despite our kiss and killer chemistry, I'm not actually dating Tristan. Whatever he thinks of me, I know he respects me and I doubt he'd deliberately hurt me. He just wouldn't want me for his future. Then again, he doesn't seem to want those models for the long-term either. Still, there's an ache in my chest as I think about him comparing me to the many women he's dated before.

"Shut up, Mark." I can't find any other words.

"I'm sorry, Kay-Kay," he says, and now there's a surprising softness in his eyes, as if he's being sincere. "I just don't want you to get hurt when he moves on to another woman."

This is the part of Mark I fell for originally, the part that seemed to care about me. "As much as I appreciate your concern …" I trail off, unsure how to respond.

"Mark, Kaylee, it's your turn," Aunt Joanne calls out.

Mark holds out his arm, and I loop my hand through his elbow. I keep my eyes forward and see Tristan watching us with an unreadable expression on his face.

"You know, I still think about you," Mark says, his voice a low murmur, only for me to hear. "My relationship with Shannon … it's not really working out."

I stumble in the sand as I whip my head in his direction but say nothing.

I glance to the side. Shannon lingering there with the family members, watching the rehearsal. If she only knew her boyfriend was all but propositioning me as she looks on.

"We worked well together. Maybe we should give it another shot."

Maybe I should've seen this coming after his behavior at the welcome dinner last night. I didn't. I don't feel anything romantic for Mark. Most of the time I only remember the frustrating things about him, not the good times. Honestly, given his parting shots at me, I assumed he felt the same way. But whether Mark is dating anyone else or not, I don't want him anymore.

We reach the arch and it's time for us to move into place, and it's a relief to step away from him.

"Great! It took four minutes for you all to reach the archway," Eric's mother says. "I'll talk to the guitar player about the timing of the song tomorrow to make sure it lines up perfectly."

"Should we practice walking back down the aisle after the ceremony?" Aunt Joanne asks.

"No," I say, not wanting to give Mark more of an opportunity to say things that make me uncomfortable. I'm still hoping to avoid a scene that steals the focus from the bride.

Tristan chuckles, and I bet he suspects the reason I don't want to walk on Mark's arm any longer than necessary.

"Yeah," Tristan says. "I think we've got it."

"I guess we're done here then," Ashley says. "I want to take a moment to thank all of you for being here with us. It means so much to us both that you were willing to spend this weekend with us and help us celebrate our love."

A murmur of *you're welcomes* comes next.

Eric kisses her cheek, and I swear I can *feel* the love between them as if it's physically emanating from their bodies, spreading through the salty ocean air. It's nice, but it also makes me ache for something like that. I want a forever love too.

Lucas places his arm over Rainey's shoulder. "We're going to head to the hotel bar and meet a friend that lives nearby for a drink if anyone wants to join us." He glances at Tristan who shakes his head. I guess he's not in the mood for socializing.

Eric turns to Ashley. "Should we check out the banquet hall before we head to our rooms?" Eric asks as Rainey and Lucas depart. "Just to make sure it's all ready to go for tomorrow?"

"Sure," Ashley says. "The event coordinator for the resort was there earlier supervising the deliveries and setting up the tables and chairs. She texted me about an hour ago, saying she was going home, and everything is done."

Tristan and I, and the rest of the bridal party, walk

back to the resort, following Eric and Ashley. The banquet hall they rented for the reception isn't far from where the ceremony will take place and we all walk into the large room. I look around, taking in the huge glass windows facing the ocean, and glance back at the pair of French doors we entered through.

Eric hits the light switch, illuminating the room, and it's beautiful. Ashley chose the colors pink and purple for the wedding. The bridesmaids' dresses are lavender while my maid-of-honor dress is the same style but a deep violet color. We'll be carrying pink bouquets of flowers while Ashley's will be a combination of pink and purple.

Here, in the banquet hall, those same colors are represented in a tasteful way. There's purple tulle draped along the high ceiling with twinkle lights and pink bows wrapped around the chairs at tables draped in crisp white tablecloths. There are white, pink, and purple balloons on the dance floor in front of a stage where the DJ's table has already been set up. As my eyes sweep over the room, I can't help feeling like something is missing, but I can't put my finger on what's wrong.

"Wait a minute …" Ashley says, stepping farther into the room, walking to the closest table. "*Where are the centerpieces?*"

Oh, no.

Within seconds, Ashley has the event coordinator on the phone, her voice shrill as she demands answers. Some awkward glances are exchanged, and Mark is the first to step away from the situation.

"Well, I think we'll head back to our room and leave you all to figure this out." Mark takes Shannon's hand.

Eric vaguely nods in his direction, his attention on his fiancée as she snaps at the coordinator on the phone.

I don't know what the other woman is saying, but Ashley's not happy.

"I don't care if it was the end of your workday. You shouldn't have just *left* without finishing. You told me the banquet hall was ready!"

I cringe. My brain goes into fix-it mode. I've dealt with plenty of last-minute screwups or mistakes in this business—something always comes up last minute— although this is extreme and unprofessional.

I take in the room, studying it from a business per- spective, and notice three boxes stacked in the corner. I rush to them as Paige also leaves the banquet hall.

The boxes contain fake flowers, mirrors, glass vas- es, and flameless votive candles. I've been in the event planning business long enough to figure out what these centerpieces are supposed to look like. Not too complicated.

Tristan watches me in silence.

I count the tables in the room. There are fifteen round tables and one long table where the wedding party will sit.

Ashley walks over to me, Eric beside her. "She left without setting up the centerpieces," she says, her cheeks flushed. "She said it was an oversight, but I think she just went home because it was the end of the day and she didn't want to deal with it anymore." Her eyes fill with tears.

That could be the case, or maybe it really was an oversight. I've seen it all, and I know there's really no point in focusing on blame. Problems need solutions.

"I can't believe this," Ashley says, shaking her head in dismay. "I'm supposed to be up early to get my nails done in the morning. And now I have to stay up dealing with this mess."

"No, you don't. I'll take care of the centerpieces." Rising to my feet, I meet her gaze.

Ashley blinks, her chin wobbles, and she throws her arms around me.

I hug her and reassure her at the same time.

"Are you sure you're okay with handling this?" Ashley asks as she pulls back. There's unmistakable hope shining in her eyes. "I know it's a lot to ask, but tomorrow is such a big day and—"

"Don't worry about it," I cut her off. "There aren't

many tables. I can put together the centerpieces tonight, no problem. Everything I need is in those boxes." I point to the open one with the flowers.

"They were supposed to be real!"

Afraid she's going to cry again, I pat her on the shoulder. "I'm going to make these look beautiful, I promise. You just go rest. You don't want dark circles under your eyes tomorrow."

"Thank you so much." Ashley steps forward to hug me again, but Eric pulls her away.

"We appreciate it, Kaylee."

I merely smile.

Everyone files out of the room except for Tristan.

"Planning to keep me company?" I ask, jokingly as I kneel down to the open box.

"No, I plan to make myself useful. I'll warn you now, though, I don't have much artistic talent."

I shoot him a grateful smile. Though it's not his problem, I appreciate the help and I'm not about to turn him down.

I pull a round mirror from one box and a glass vase from the other. "This is a basic setup." The vase sits on the mirror with the purple pebbles in the bottom. Then, we fill it with the fake pink flowers and water. We'll surround the vase with the votive candles on the mirror and they can be turned on tomorrow at the beginning of the reception."

Tristan nods along as I explain. "All right, put me to work."

I have Tristan unpack the mirrors from the box, while I find glass cleaner in a nearby closet. I make sure the mirrors are spotless, handing them over to Tristan to place in the center of each table. It takes a little time, but I don't mind because I have good company.

He tells me all about running the nightclub and it's less exciting than I imagined. "I swear, I spend more time in my office doing paperwork than anything else."

I scoff. "Come on. That can't be true. Every time I come in, you're swaggering around the VIP section, flashing your charming smile at everyone like you're king of the world."

"You think my smile is charming?" He waggles his eyebrows, and I snicker as I shove him playfully. "But yeah, I spend about fifteen minutes strutting around like I own the place—"

"Because you do," I interrupt.

"*But* most of my energy is spent dealing with things like invoices and staff scheduling and insurance. That's a lot of time stuck in a windowless room where the bobblehead on the corner of my desk practically vibrates with the continuous thump of the bass from the loud music."

"A bobblehead?" I exclaim like an excited child. "What kind?"

"It's Chewbacca," he admits.

"From *Star Trek*?"

He scowls at me like I've committed a murder. "It's *Star Wars*. Good Lord, woman. You're killing me."

I roll my eyes, even as my lips curl in a smile. "Okay, okay. I didn't know you were a closet nerd."

"Hey, I don't hide it. You think a nerd can't run a nightclub?"

I trail my eyes over his sculpted body. I'm not usually one to judge a book by its cover, but I have to admit I wouldn't expect a nerd to look like *him*.

"And what about your job?" he asks as we move on to filling the vases. "Have you always wanted to be an event planner?"

"Not necessarily, but it's something I've always enjoyed doing. From planning my own birthday parties as a kid to being on the prom committee in high school, I love coming up with ways to make people happy at a party, to keep them entertained."

"And corporate event planning? How did that happen?" he asks, as he pours water into the vases where I've placed the flowers, moving slowly and carefully so he doesn't spill a single drop.

"Well, that was all Rainey. She did her research on

other companies in the area and which type we were more likely to be successful in. She saw a space for us in corporate and we started with smaller companies and thanks to word of mouth, we have worked our way up to the bigger ones."

He nods. "Like the Miami Thunder's anniversary season this year?"

"Yes, though Rainey ran with that one since I had the charity fundraiser we all attended a few months ago, remember?"

"I do."

I let out a laugh.

"What's so amusing?"

"Oh, just remembering how my assistant and I worked overtime on that one." I hesitate, then decide I trust him with my true self. "I have severe ADD," I tell him. "I'm good at the creative parts, but need someone to keep me organized and on time." I bite down on the inside of my cheek, finding my admission embarrassing, mostly because Mark did.

"Yet you made the best of the hand you were dealt. Look at you, one of the top-rated event planners in Miami." His gaze meets mine and I find understanding not judgment there.

"I appreciate that," I tell him. "A lot goes into making things work for and not against me. Setting alarm clocks earlier, paying my assistant very well to stay on top of things, too."

"Hey. Don't sell yourself short." Tristan steps close to me, his hands cupping my cheeks. "You're you, and I like *you*. A lot. In fact, I find you sexy as hell."

My heart flutters as he tilts my head back, and my lips part, eyes closing. I'm lightheaded already when his lips brush against mine and I let out a needy groan. I slide my hands up the back of his neck and pull him closer, deepening the kiss and telling him without words that I want more.

The kiss goes on until he lifts his head, and says in a husky, desire-laden voice, "Please tell me we're finished in here."

"We're all set."

He grabs my hand and we rush to our room upstairs.

# CHAPTER EIGHT

## *Tristan*

T HE HOTEL ROOM door slams against the wall as we stumble into the room, our hands pulling at each other's clothes and lips locked together. Desire rages through me and I barely manage to kick the door closed, shutting out the rest of the world as I get lost in the taste and feel of Kaylee. Thanks to her flowy skirt, it's easy to strip her down to her underwear and pull off her tank top, leaving her in a mouthwatering, barely-there bra and panties set.

I pick her up with ease and carry her to our single but very large bed. As I stride across the floor, she kicks off her sandals, adding them to a pile on the floor. I lay her down on the bed and hover over her, then set my lips on her neck, nipping her skin. Her body is all feminine curves and soft skin, and my cock *aches* with the need to be buried inside of her. I don't know if I've ever wanted a woman this much before. It's all-consuming, my entire body in tune with hers as I grind my erection into her core.

The light from the lamp on the nightstand is dim,

but it's bright enough to see her perky nipples are poking through the fabric of her white bra. It's nothing fancy but the way it barely contains her full breasts makes it sexy as hell.

She arches her back as I reach behind her to pop it open and bare her breasts to my heated gaze. Bringing them together with my hands, I bury my face between them, inhaling her sweet scent as I lave her soft skin with my tongue.

"Tristan," she moans, burying her fingers in my hair. "More, please …"

I take a nipple into my mouth, swirling my tongue around the hard bud even as my hands are busy yanking down her panties. I'm still wearing my pants, but I'll take care of that soon enough. For now, I keep my mouth on her breast and I place my hand between her legs.

She's soaked, and my cock jerks in my boxer briefs as I sink a long finger inside her. She whimpers, encouraging me, and I pump my finger in and out as I graze my teeth over her nipple. A full-body shudder moves through her.

Then, I add a second finger, and she cries out. "Oh God, yes! It feels so good, Tristan. *So good.*"

I'd planned to wait until she came at least once before I took her, but I can't. I need to feel her warm wetness around my cock.

Luckily, I usually carry a condom in my wallet, something my grandpa taught me in his failed attempt to give me a sex ed talk when I was fifteen. It was mortifying then, but now, I'm just glad I don't have to break away from Kaylee to look around my suitcase.

Leaning over the side of the bed, I grab my pants, pull out my wallet, and find the condom. I roll it on, my eyes skimming over Kaylee's hot body. I can't wait to feel those long legs around me and I grasp her hips, pulling her closer. Her thighs part, and I can see her sex glistening in the dim light.

"So wet for me, baby. I bet you've been thinking about this all night, haven't you?"

Before she can reply, I line myself up at her entrance and jerk my hips forward, burying myself deep inside her in one rough thrust.

She lets out a breathy cry of surprise and pleasure, pitched low and tinged with an edge of desperate need. I'll think of that sound often in the future. She's tight and wet around me, and I don't waste time with slow and gentle. My need is too great, hers too, by the way her fingernails dig into my shoulders, and her hips lift to meet my forceful thrusts.

I brace my arms tighter on either side of her, my hands pressing into the mattress as my hips slap against hers. An overwhelming sense of possession fills me as I pound into her, bending my head to claim her mouth in a kiss that turns into a tangling of our tongues.

"I knew you'd feel good, sweetheart, I've been thinking about this all day. Ever since I woke up to your hot body draped over me this morning," I tell her.

"Tristan," she moans my name in the most beautiful way, "I'm close. I'm so … so …"

I thrust once more and she comes with a gasp, clenching around me as she soars through her climax. Feeling her squeeze tight triggers my release and I drive myself in deep, my body trembling from the power of my climax.

I lose track of time and place, and when my orgasm has passed, I collapse onto Kaylee. Not wanting to crush her, I roll to the side, slipping out of her. I roll over and walk to the bathroom, making quick work of getting rid of the condom before returning to bed.

I turn off the lamp on the nightstand, plunging us into near-total darkness. Kaylee curls into my side, her head resting on my chest and our legs tangled together.

She fits against me just right. After a moment, our breathing syncs up. Kaylee starts tracing random patterns on my chest with the tips of her fingers, while I absentmindedly stroke her back.

"Well," I say, "this weekend ended up being a lot more fun than I expected."

Kaylee laughs. "It's certainly been full of surprises so far."

She's quiet for a moment, and when she speaks again, her voice is more serious. "You know, I've always been attracted to you. But I never would have made a move."

I slide my fingers up and twirl them in her long hair. "I guess we got lucky the timing was right this weekend." I don't like the idea of missing out on this connection between us.

"We did," she murmurs.

I think about the circumstances that brought us here, starting with the rooming situation and leading to fake dating to keep Mark from giving her a hard time. "What happened between you and Mark anyway? Why did you break up?"

Kaylee sighs. "Mark is … emotionally stunted. I know he's capable of love because he's very close to his mom and sister, and he *definitely* loves his job. A little too much, really. He's a workaholic. Maybe I could have dealt with the long days when he was working extra hours and the canceled dates because of some important issue if I knew he truly cared about me. If he ever *once* said he loved me."

"He never said it? But weren't you together for,

like, two years?" I ask, surprised.

"Yep," she says, popping the P. "I said it, but he never said it back. And he was so afraid of real commitment that he wouldn't even discuss emotions. When I tried to talk about planning a real future together, he shut me down right away. He said he just wanted to focus on the present. Eventually, I had to admit to myself that I was wasting my time."

"It seems like he hasn't taken the breakup well."

She lets out an adorable snorting sound. "No kidding. He showed more emotion when I ended the relationship than he did the whole time we were together. It wasn't pretty. All of a sudden, my every flaw became a huge problem, a reason no one else would ever want to be with me. But none of them were too much for *him* to handle, because he was *very* clear I should just keep dating him. Needless to say, I declined."

"It sounds like you made the right call. Some men just aren't built for relationships."

She nods against me. "The worst part is, I always felt so uncertain with Mark. I never truly knew where I stood or where things were going."

I tighten my arm around her. "You deserve someone better."

*I* could treat her better. I'm about to speak when I realize her breathing is getting deep and even. She's about to fall asleep and I'm getting tired myself, so I close my eyes and bask in the peace I feel with her in my arms.

# CHAPTER NINE

## *Tristan*

THE DAY OF the wedding is chaotic from the moment it begins. I volunteer to run to the tux rental shop when it turns out we're somehow missing a pair of cuff links, Lucas's shoes are the wrong size, and there's a small white spot on the bottom of my jacket that looks like someone might have spilled bleach on it.

I appreciate the break away from the craziness of the wedding preparations, and by the time I return, it's nearly time for the ceremony to begin. We all line up in place, and I wait with Paige, the bridesmaid I'm walking with, but my eyes keep drifting to Kaylee. All the women in the bridal party are wearing the same style of dress, but hers is a darker purple, identifying her as the maid of honor. The front has a deep V-neck that shows off the swell of her breasts and I can't stop thinking about a repeat of last night.

Mark comes up to her, taking his position beside her, and I have to work to keep the scowl off my face. I didn't like seeing them walk arm in arm last night, and I doubt I'll enjoy it any more today. What I like even less is the way Mark looks at her, as if he realizes he made a mistake and has lost something precious.

But as we stand under the archway, Kaylee's eyes lock on mine and that's enough to give me peace. And for me to come to a stunning realization. I don't want this to end. This *thing* we have between us isn't fake for me anymore, and I want to see where it goes after the wedding weekend is over.

Before I can contemplate further, the music starts and it's time to walk down the aisle. The ceremony runs smoothly and after, we all head inside for the reception. When I get to the wedding party's assigned table, I discover I'm not seated next to Kaylee. Instead, I'm sitting between Mark and Lucas while Kaylee is between Ashley and Rainey. I console myself with the fact that at least she's not next to Mark. I'd hate for him to ruin her day by pressuring her or giving her a hard time.

After we eat, the dinging of a fork against a glass of champagne rings out, quieting the room. The DJ hands Kaylee the microphone, and she flashes a bright smile at everyone before she begins her maid-of-honor speech.

"Hi, everyone. My name is Kaylee, and I'm the maid of honor. Ashley is my cousin, but in a lot of ways, I've always thought of her as the sister I never had. We were thick as thieves growing up, and now that we're adults, we're even closer. So, I know this woman better than most people, and I can confidently say I've never seen her so happy.

"Eric completes her in a way that you read about in books, the ones with swoon-worthy heroes. Ashley and Eric share the kind of love people think isn't real until they see it for themselves, and that's because they're right for each other in every way. When you find that person, the one that fits you perfectly, you hold on tight and never let go. And that's why we're here today. This wedding is the beginning of a long and happy life for one of the best couples I know, so please raise your glass to Ashley and Eric."

There is applause and we all drink to Kaylee's toast, as she hands her microphone over to Mark. His speech is similar to Kaylee's. He talks about the importance of finding the right person and what a good match Ashley and Eric are. But his eyes shift from the crowd to look directly at Kaylee, and my free hand curls into a fist. "I commend Eric for winning Ashley's heart," Mark says. "After all, it's important to seize the moment and make sure the woman you love knows how much she matters to you." His attention moves back to Ashley and Eric as he also calls for everyone to raise their glass and toast the happy couple.

I'm waiting for my chance to go to Kaylee. When, finally, the dancing starts, I rise and walk over to her, holding out my arm. "Can I have this dance?"

Her face lights up, and she takes my hand, letting me pull her out of her seat. "Are you sure you can slow dance?" she asks teasingly as we head to the dance floor. "It's not like the twerking I see in your club."

I laugh. "I'll have you know I'm a very accomplished ballroom dancer. My grandmother wanted me to learn how to do it, so she insisted I take lessons for a whole year." I can't say I liked it at the time, but it's come in handy as an adult.

"You're just full of surprises," she tells me.

I agree. I'm surprised by the possessiveness I feel toward her after Mark's little speech. I've never really had that reaction to a woman before. It's one of the reasons I've ended so many relationships. But now? I want Kaylee to be mine and for everyone to know it. I hold her body tight against me as we sway on the dance floor, hoping Mark sees and understands he's missed his chance. Not that I'm paying any attention to where he is. My focus is on Kaylee and the way her smile lights up the room. With her in my arms, all I can think about is me taking off that sexy dress later tonight, before I lose all patience and strip her naked.

For now, I'm happy to stand close, and we dance

to two songs. The third is just beginning when she stops moving on the dance floor. "I need a drink," she says.

We head to our table, my hand on her lower back, when I see Eric. "I'm going to talk to the groom," I tell Kaylee. "I'll be right back."

"Go ahead. I'll be guzzling water at my seat," she says, laughing.

Aware I plan to slip away early tonight to take Kaylee back to our room, I want to wish my good friend all the best. Once I have that taken care of, it's time for the bride and groom to cut the cake, so we all gather around the special table, watching as they hold the knife together and slice into the white confection.

I take it all in, but I also glance around, wondering where Kaylee disappeared to. When I don't see her, I decide to track her down. After Eric holds out a piece of cake to Ashley, I'm ready to go when someone touches my arm.

Turning, I see a stranger beside me. The woman is probably in her mid-twenties and wearing a little too much perfume. It overwhelms me as she stands so close.

"I'm sorry to bother you, but you just look so familiar to me. Have we met before?" she asks, batting her eyelashes along with the bad pickup line, but maybe I'm wrong.

"I don't think so. My name is Tristan."

She leans in closer. "Cindy. I'm a friend of Ashley's. But I don't know anyone else here. Maybe you can be my friend?" she asks coyly.

There's no mistaking the look in her eyes now, and she's definitely not asking for friendship. I open my mouth to turn her down, already starting to pull my arm away, when the small hairs on the back of my neck stand up. Lifting my head, I see the crowd around us has shifted, and ten feet away, Kaylee is standing, watching us. Her pretty eyes aren't sparkling and I know she's misinterpreting what she sees.

Especially when she turns away and walks in the other direction.

"Excuse me," I say to Cindy, and weave my way through the mingling guests in search of my girl.

# CHAPTER TEN

## *Kaylee*

I WATCH A woman openly flirt with Tristan and feel an uncomfortable twisting pain in my stomach. Though I can't hear what's being said from this distance, the woman looks up at Tristan through her eyelashes, her body angled toward him in a way that's obviously meant to draw his attention.

We aren't in a relationship, but he did promise to be my date this weekend. I trust him not to betray me in that way, but I can't help the feeling of jealousy that weaves through me. I also wonder if that's the kind of woman to hold and keep his attention. She seems like his type based on his past girlfriends, but those never stuck, so who knows? It's none of my business as long as he doesn't embarrass me in front of everyone who thinks we're dating. Or so I tell myself.

Before I can get my emotions under control, Tristan looks my way. I don't get a chance to school my features, to appear unaffected the way I want to. Knowing myself, I'm sure my unwarranted hurt feelings are showing in my face, so I turn away.

The cake cutting is done, which means we're almost finished with the traditional wedding activities. The only thing left is the bouquet toss and then more dancing. I decide to go the bathroom to collect myself. I just need a chance to tuck away these dark feelings so I can be the maid of honor my cousin deserves and because I need to compose myself before someone asks me what's wrong.

Or maybe I could just slip away for the night. Ashely is surrounded by family and friends. I did the toast and helped make sure this wedding went off without a hitch. We're nearly three hours into the reception now. Surely, it'd be okay to head back up to my room … which I'm sharing with Tristan. Maybe the bathroom is a better choice, for now.

I walk to the isolated hallway just outside the banquet hall where the bathrooms are located when a hand lands on my shoulder and spins me around. I gasp and look up into Tristan's face.

His intense gaze is focused on me and a slight frown mars his face. "Where are you running off to, sweetheart?"

The damn nickname gives me butterflies every time he uses it. Right now, in the aftermath of his moment with that woman, it's the last thing I want to feel. "The bathroom." I gesture behind me, breaking eye contact.

His large hand covers my fingers which I'm twisting nervously. He stops the edgy motion and with the knuckle of his other hand, he lifts my chin until I have to meet his gaze or admit I'm trying not to.

Tristan's brow furrows as he studies me, like he's trying to solve a puzzle. "Tell me why you're upset," he says.

"I'm not," I say, but my quick reply makes it clear I'm lying, and his frown deepens.

"You have to know, I wasn't interested in that woman. She was hitting on me, but I wasn't going to—"

"It's fine," I cut him off. "It's none of my business. We're fake dating and—"

"It definitely is your business," he says, his tone sharp and his eyes burning into mine. "It's your business because there's only one woman I want, and it's *you*," he says in a softer voice.

He kisses me and all of the doubt melts away. He places his hands on my hips, jerking my body into his so I can feel his erection pressing into my stomach. A jagged moan escapes me, and I part my lips, but he pulls away instead of deepening the kiss. Pressing his forehead against mine, he stares at me with eyes that have grown dark.

"Do you think they'd miss us if we left the party now?" he asks, his voice gruff and raw.

My heart is beating hard in my chest as I reply. "I was thinking the same thing."

He takes my hand and pulls me into the lobby. "Come on, Kaylee. I'm going to *show* you there's no one in my mind but you."

Ten minutes later, we're back in our hotel room. Last night, our joining was rough and fast, an explosion of need. Now, Tristan is more restrained but no less passionate as he kisses me thoroughly, his tongue deep inside my mouth. He slowly pulls down the zipper at the back of my dress and runs his knuckles down my spine, the light touch setting off every nerve ending in my body.

I shudder, my head falling back. Tristan's mouth moves along my jaw, and he nips my earlobe before continuing to kiss down my neck, letting out a low groan. "How do you feel and taste so damn *good?*"

I know he doesn't expect an answer and that's a good thing because my brain is scrambled by the desire pulsing through my veins with each frantic beat of my heart.

The dress pools at my feet, leaving me in only a pair of lacy black panties. The cut of the dress didn't allow for a bra, and the fit provided enough support to make one unnecessary.

"*Fuck*, you're gorgeous and all I want."

My skin tingles as he sweeps his gaze down my

body, and in that moment, I believe him. I believe I'm all he wants, even if it's just for tonight, or maybe just for this weekend. No matter how strong the connection between us feels, I can't forget about how he never finds any woman enough to continue in a relationship. But I'm not going to let his past ruin what we do together tonight.

As he pulls me into the bathroom, I push all thoughts of tomorrow away. He's still fully dressed in his tuxedo, but he shrugs out of the jacket and starts unbuttoning his shirt, revealing the broad expanse of his chest. He starts to unbutton and unzip his pants and my panties grow damp at the sight.

His gaze meets mine and a sexy smirk lifts the corners of his mouth. "Baby, if you keep looking at me like that, I'm going to lose all self-control."

"Good," I tell him, and he chuckles.

"No loss of control tonight. I want to take my time with you."

I'm not sure what he has planned, but the fact that we're in the bathroom gives me a pretty good idea. As soon as he's naked, his thick erection jutting out from his hips, he turns to the shower and starts the water. While he adjusts the temperature, I shed my panties and kick off my heels.

Getting impatient, I come up behind him, so that only inches separate us when he finally gets the temperature just right and turns back around to face me. He didn't hear me approaching, so he lets out a grunt of surprise that shifts into a gasp as I reach out and grip his cock in my hand.

"Kaylee …"

The husky plea in his voice makes me ache for him, but I agree with his idea of taking our time. I stroke up and down his shaft while we stand in front of the shower, peppering kisses over his chest and neck, feeling the cords of muscle flex beneath my mouth.

Steam starts filling the bathroom, and Tristan places a hand on my wrist to stop my movements. I pout and he chuckles, then pulls me into the shower and *drops to his knees.* Water beats down on his wide back as he shifts and moves me so my back is pressed against the tile wall.

My pulse is racing at the thought of what comes next. He lifts my leg over his shoulder and buries his face between my thighs, licking from my entrance to my clit, his gaze on mine, like he *needs* to see my reaction. I cry out at the slick feel of his tongue and squirm as he sucks on the sensitive tight bud. Pinning my hips to the wall, he growls against my pussy, the vibrations sending an electric jolt up my spine.

Heat engulfs me, need and pleasure spiraling in a way I've never felt before. He knows his way around a woman's body. No tentative moves, no hesitation. He ravages me and I grab a handful of his hair and rock myself against his face.

"So sweet," Tristan mutters. "Come for me, sweetheart. I want to taste it all."

His tongue flicks my clit and I moan as he slides two fingers inside me. Finally, I climax hard, a scream ripping from my throat and echoing in the shower stall. I should be embarrassed, but I can't be. Not when he seems to enjoy this as much as I am.

When I finish trembling, he rises to his feet and kisses me, allowing me to taste myself on his tongue. It's the most erotic thing I've ever experienced. He slides a condom on, one that I didn't notice him bring into the shower with us, and lifts one leg off the ground so it's wrapped around his hip as he sinks into me, filling me so deep I'll feel him for days.

Needing something to hold on to, I grip his arms hard. "Tristan!"

He pulls out and slams back into me. There's nothing but pleasure and need between us now. He's taking me hard and fast, panting as he buries his face in my neck. His hands grab my ass, kneading the flesh and guiding me up and down as he moves.

I don't expect to come again so soon, but there's something about the angle he hits that makes my entire body sing. I shake as I arch my back, rubbing my breasts against his chest.

"Come again for me, Kaylee," Tristan commands. "I need to feel it. Your tight pussy drives me crazy."

His dirty words do the trick, and a heady sensation envelops me as I fall apart again. This time, Tristan is right there with me, his body taut as he groans my name in my ear.

# CHAPTER ELEVEN

## *Kaylee*

I WAKE UP with body aches and a smile on my face, last night with Tristan fresh in my mind. He's wrapped around me, his chest pressed to my back and his face buried in my hair. Each time he exhales, it tickles my neck, but he feels so warm and good I can't bring myself to care.

I'm *happy*.

I can't remember feeling this good, this satisfied, this elated … ever.

Then, I remember what day it is. *Sunday*. The wedding weekend is almost over. The only event left is a thank-you brunch being hosted by Ashley and Eric. Then, we'll all head back to our real lives, and my heart feels heavy at the thought. I've had the best weekend I could have imagined, which is incredible considering how it started with me dateless. Before Tristan stepped in.

That was kindness, but the rest of it? The snorkeling, hanging out on the beach, him helping with the centerpieces, the long talks … and the sex. That was something more, for me, at least, which is the problem. My emotions are involved, but I can't let myself read too much into his actions. Not everyone is like me. I'm the type to seriously date the men I sleep with. I look for that spark and try to coax it into a flame. And I've never felt for any man what I feel for Tristan. But I warned myself going into this, it was a fun weekend only, and I plan to stick to that promise.

I can let myself dwell on the fact that I've developed real feelings for a man I knew wasn't emotionally available, or I can take the good memories from this weekend and remember them fondly without feeling sad about what could have been. The latter is the far better option. The one Tristan deserves.

I softly turn in Tristan's arms until I'm facing him. He's still asleep, and I brush my lips over his cheek before getting out of bed without waking him up. As much as I want more time, the best choice is to leave before he wakes up. No messy goodbyes. No forcing him to feel obligated to explain it was one weekend only.

I dress and quietly throw my things into my suitcase and walk to the door. Pausing just before I leave the room, I look at Tristan's sleeping form and smile.

It really was a great weekend.

Heading down the hall, I stop by Ashley and Eric's room and knock on the door. Ashley pulls it open, wearing a terrycloth robe with mascara smudged under her eyes. Her hair is a mess, but she looks purely happy, and I'm glad.

"Hey!" she says. "What's up? Why do you have your suitcase with you?"

"I'm going to take off a little early," I say.

"Why?" Ashley doesn't look upset that I'll be skipping the brunch, but she's concerned.

"I'm just exhausted from the weekend, and I want to get back home a little early so I'm well-rested for work tomorrow." It's a lie, and not even a good one, but I don't want to bring my fake relationship drama to my cousin on her first day as a happily married woman. She doesn't need that today.

"Okay," Ashley says, and I'm not sure if she believes me, but I appreciate that she's not pushing me for a real answer.

Hugging her, I congratulate her once again and leave the resort.

During the drive home, my determination to look back on my time with Tritan as nothing more than a fond memory wavers. I want to be as casual about the whole thing as I'm sure he is, but with each mile I put between us, the more my chest aches with the certainty that my feelings for Tristan are too strong to get over easily.

I have no choice and one day, I'll look back knowing I'm over the man that was never mine to begin with.

I hope.

# CHAPTER TWELVE

## *Tristan*

B RUNCH IS A much bigger event than the previous meals we've had in the resort's restaurant. Instead of it just being the wedding party, the thank-you brunch is for all the wedding guests who attended. Eric's parents reserved half the tables in the restaurant, and when I arrive, most of them are full.

I look around for Kaylee. She wasn't in bed when I woke up this morning and I was disappointed. Though I texted her to find out where she'd gone, she didn't respond. Assuming she made plans with Rainey or Ashley this morning and forgot to mention it to me, I showered, dressed, and headed downstairs. But both women are here, and Kaylee is nowhere to be seen. I walk to the table where Rainey and Lucas are sitting with Paige and Cindy, the woman who was hitting on me last night. I don't give her a second glance as I focus on Rainey.

"Hey, you two. Have you seen Kaylee this morning?" I ask, interrupting her conversation with Lucas. It's rude, but I'm worried. Kaylee should be here. "I haven't been able to find her this morning."

Rainey frowns and looks around as if just realizing Kaylee isn't present. "No, I haven't spoken to her today."

"I did," Ashley says from the table behind me, where she's sitting with Mark and his girlfriend. "She came by my room this morning to tell me she was heading home early."

I frown. "What? When was this?"

Ashley shrugs. "Maybe an hour ago? She didn't tell you?"

"No. No, she didn't." *Why the hell didn't she wake me before she left?*

She didn't even say goodbye. We both live in Miami and have mutual friends, so it's not like we'll never see each other again, but I still thought we'd have a conversation about where this thing between us is going. It couldn't have meant nothing to her. She's not a casual-relationship type of woman, which is why I was surprised things went as far as they did between us. But I didn't think to question it, assuming we could talk Sunday morning.

Mark snickers. "That's rough, man. Kaylee might've dumped me, but at least she had the decency to do it to my face, like I mattered. She *ghosted you.*"

"Shut up," I snap, aware we're drawing attention. "You don't know anything about me and Kaylee."

"I know enough. I warned her about you."

I stiffen. Surprise rushes through me, but then again, I shouldn't be shocked Mark would try and sabotage things between me and Kaylee. "What did you say to her?" I take a step toward him, and he jumps to his feet, while Eric stares back and forth between us, clearly concerned he's going to have to break up a fight. "What exactly did you *warn* her about?" I ask.

"Yeah, Mark," his girlfriend says, her voice hard. "What did you tell her?"

Mark hesitates, but there are too many eyes on him for him to back down now without losing face.

He shrugs. "I just told her what I overheard you saying to Lucas about how she's not your usual type." His shoulders lower and he's lost some of his confidence, but his eyes are hard as he glares at me. "Kaylee's the type to settle down, you know. Everyone knows you're not."

"I know more about Kaylee than you do, no matter how much longer you dated her," I say, taking a step closer. Only about a foot of space separates us now, and I see Eric and Lucas both tense, both prepared to step in if things get physical. "And I know you blew it by refusing to commit to her, but I won't make that same mistake."

"You won't want to settle for Kaylee," he says, but

he must see the sincerity in my eyes because he doesn't sound so sure.

I cock an eyebrow. "I wouldn't be settling. I'd be lucky to have her, and unlike you, I'm going to make sure she knows it. So, get rid of any thoughts you have of reconciling with her because she's my girl now."

Mark glares at me, but I turn away, done with this conversation. Besides, based on the angry look on his girlfriend's face, he has more important things to worry about and I'm guessing that relationship will end soon.

I clap Eric on the shoulder. "Congratulations, man. You're a lucky guy. Now, I've got to go find Kaylee."

"Good luck," Ashley calls out as I hurry out of the restaurant.

I have a feeling that luck is exactly what I'm going to need.

# CHAPTER THIRTEEN

## *Kaylee*

M Y APARTMENT IS a mess. Sitting on the couch in my living room, I look around at the clutter. There are books stacked on the end table that should be on the bookshelf, a pile of unopened mail on the kitchen counter, and a basket of clean laundry resting on the other end of the couch that needs to be put away.

I try to muster up the energy to deal with it but can't. I'm too busy having second thoughts about leaving this morning. I've been home for two hours, and I can't stop thinking about Tristan and what I could have done differently. Like telling him how I felt.

I don't know if he would be open to a serious relationship because I didn't ask, and that's what tortures me. I was too afraid of rejection. The string of women on Tristan's arm over the last couple of years didn't help, but most of all, I realized while driving home that I've been carrying around baggage from my relationship with Mark. I don't have feelings for him anymore, but at one point, loved him and he never treated me right, then said awful, humiliating things when I broke up with him. I know now he was trying to hurt me to assuage his ego but for a long time, I wondered if I was that unlovable like he said.

With Tristan, the spark was there, and when he kissed me, I *felt* like there could be so much more between us. And I knew he had feelings for me. I just didn't think he'd want more. Groaning, I rub my temples. All of this overthinking is giving me a headache.

I stand up, planning to grab some Tylenol from the bathroom, but a knock on my apartment door stops me. I'm not expecting anyone, so I look through the peephole and gasp when I see Tristan.

I open the door to see him standing with a white plastic bag in one hand and a serious look on his face.

"Tristan?" I say his name like I'm not sure he's real, as if all my ruminating conjured him up.

"It's me. I thought you might be hungry since you skipped brunch," he says simply, lifting the bag in his hand. It's then I notice the logo printed on the side.

"You brought me sushi from On a Roll?" I ask as he brushes by me on his way inside. Like he belongs here.

My mind is reeling. When I left the resort, I thought I'd have time before I saw him again, time to get my emotions under control and my head on straight about what this weekend really meant. But now, he's here, and I'm at a loss.

He nods. "You said it's your favorite."

I did say that, but I didn't realize he was paying enough attention to remember the name of the specific restaurant. The fact that he not only remembered it but bought some for me causes a warm glow to fill my chest, replacing the emptiness I've been feeling since I left him at the resort.

"I ... I don't know what to say. I mean, I didn't expect you to ..."

"I know you didn't," he says, placing the bag of food on the coffee table in front of the couch. "I'm not sure what you did expect since you took off without saying goodbye, but I doubt you thought I'd follow you home." He appears calm, his body relaxed, no tension that I can see.

"How did you know where I live?" I ask.

He smirks. "We have people in common, sweetheart." He takes a seat on the couch, right next to the neglected basket of laundry, and starts unloading containers of sushi onto the table.

Just minutes ago, I was debating whether or not I'd made a huge mistake by leaving him behind without a conversation, and now he's *here*.

"Tristan, what's going on?" I ask, wondering if this

is the opportunity I denied myself earlier.

He glances over and lifts an eyebrow. "What do you mean?"

"Not to be rude, but why are you here?" I ask.

"Where else would your boyfriend be?" he replies, and doesn't even stop opening the sushi containers.

"You were my fake boyfriend," I remind him, unsure of why I'm objecting to something I want so badly.

He stands, take two steps, and suddenly he's directly in front of me, reaching out and pulling me flush against his hard body. "Does this really feel fake to you, sweetheart?"

Without a thought, I melt into him, breathing in completely for the first time in hours. "It feels real," I manage to say around the lump in my throat. "I didn't think you did serious relationships."

"I said it wasn't worth the hassle. But that's when the woman isn't the right one for me. And you never asked me what I wanted. If you had, you'd know that I'm *very* interested in one with you."

I pull back just enough to look into his eyes. He meets my gaze head-on, hiding nothing from me. "I just want you to know what you're getting into with me. It's just that … I'm a mess. Literally." I gesture to my cluttered apartment.

It was the biggest complaint that Mark had about

me. He said no one wants to spend time in a messy apartment, and if I had any self-respect, I'd do better to keep it clean. I know he's a jerk, but I also know he had a point. I know my issues and, as a result, I'm not very organized. But ever since Mark, I wonder if it would bother another man too.

There are other things, too.

"I'm also late a lot. Like, most of the time. The wedding was different. I was on a specific schedule, which helps. I also tend to be a daydreamer. Mark always said my head was in the clouds. I mean, I get so wrapped up in my creative projects sometimes that I forget things. Like eating."

Tristan looks like he's trying not to laugh. "Is that it? The end of your great list of reasons I should walk away?"

I nibble on my bottom lip and twist my fingers together, not sure what to say or do. I just cut myself open and showed him the ugly side of being with me, and he's acting like it's a joke.

"I'm serious," I say, my voice cracking as I try to rein in my emotional reaction. "It bothered Mark. Better you know now before you get in deep with me."

Tristan's smirk vanishes, and he pulls me into him again, this time hugging me so tight I can barely breathe. But I don't want him to stop.

"Those things you just listed? That's your list of flaws? Come on, sweetheart. There's nothing that's a deal-breaker. So, you're not perfect. Who is? In fact, perfect sounds boring. I'd much rather have you the way you are."

Something shifts inside of me at those words. I can't say Mark's reactions don't matter to me because my relationship with him will always be a part of the past that shaped me into who I am today. But I *can* say Tristan's acceptance of me, flaws and all, makes me realize Mark was overly critical. And mean.

"Thank you," I tell him.

With a warm smile, he cups my cheek and I lean into his touch. "Does this mean we're a real couple now?" I ask cheekily.

Tristan's eyes gleam with happiness. "Well, I fell hard for you, so I hope so."

His words are good enough for me. Lifting onto my toes, I press a kiss to his lips. Hopefully, the first of many more to come.

# EPILOGUE

## *Tristan*

*One Year Later*

I FINISH MY scotch and check my watch, seeing I've been waiting at the restaurant for twenty minutes. The bartender is lingering nearby, and I know he's going to come over soon to offer me another drink. It's a tempting thought because I feel unusually nervous. But I want to have a completely clear head when Kaylee arrives. It's more important tonight than ever.

I glance at my phone, checking one of Midnight's social media pages. Tonight, Lucas is running things while a very popular local band plays at the club for the first time. According to the social media posts and tags, it's going well.

Satisfied, I tuck my phone in my pocket just as familiar blonde hair catches my eye.

Kaylee's arrived. Her gaze meets mine and she glances down, feeling guilty for being late. No matter how many times I tell her I expect it, she feels bad.

She passes the hostess stand, then walks over to the bar where I'm waiting for our table to be ready.

"Oh my gosh, I'm so sorry," she says, obviously flustered.

She wasn't lying when she told me she's often late for things. After a year together, I've come to realize it's especially bad when she's busy with work. Her beautiful, creative mind gets so wrapped up in whatever she's doing that time fades away for her.

She's in the middle of planning a large party for a corporation that's used her company before, so she's got plenty on her to-do list.

"I didn't mean to be late."

I laugh as I rise and press a kiss to her cheek. I'd normally pull her in closer for a proper kiss hello, but I'm worried that if her body is pressed against mine, she'll feel the little box in my pocket and tonight's surprise will be ruined.

"Don't worry, sweetheart. I expect it by now."

Kaylee gasps and slaps my arm, and I just grin at her.

She knows I don't mean anything by my comment. Some people might be bothered by her running late, but I find it charming. She's not intentionally thoughtless. She's just a little scatterbrained sometimes. A year ago, she told me Mark called her a daydreamer like it's a bad thing. I don't see it that way. Yes, she gets carried away sometimes when her mind latches onto a creative idea, but that's what I'm here for. I keep her grounded and take care of her in any way she needs me to. And at work, she has Alissa, her assistant to keep her on point.

"We didn't lose our reservation, did we?" she asks, looking more guilty than before.

"No. I told you to be here a half hour before the time of the reservation."

Her mouth opens wide. "So, I'm actually ten minutes early?"

I laugh again. "Sure, baby. Think of it that way if you'd like. We both know you're late."

Kaylee playfully pouts, poking out her full bottom lip, and I can't resist leaning forward to kiss it.

Her blue eyes grow darker as her cheeks flush. The sexual chemistry between the two of us is just as potent as ever, and I look forward to getting her home later to fulfill the unspoken promise that's thick in the air.

"Hayes, party of two," the hostess calls out, and we step apart.

We live together in an apartment we picked out four months ago, so there will be plenty of time to ravage each other later tonight. And I hope we'll have something to celebrate.

That thought brings the jitters back to the surface.

We're seated at a table near a window with a view of Miami's skyline. The sun has long set, so everything is lit up and alive. It's an amazing view and the main reason I picked this restaurant.

"Look, I can see Midnight from here," Kaylee says, and I nod, too busy thinking about what's coming up at the end of the meal to be much of a conversationalist.

Of course, Kaylee knows me too well not to notice something's bothering me. She tilts her head to the side as she studies me with sharp eyes. "Are you okay?"

"Of course. Why wouldn't I be?"

My mouth is suddenly very dry, so I take a sip of the water already on the table for us.

"I don't know," Kaylee says, still watching me. "Do you feel okay?"

I make an impulsive decision, just like I did the night I offered to be Kaylee's fake date for Ashley and Eric's wedding. That worked out pretty well, so I'm going with my gut.

"You know what … I was going to wait until the end of dinner for this, but I just decided I can't wait."

I reach across the table and take her left hand. As I look into her eyes, the restaurant fades into the background. "Kaylee, over the past year, I've gotten to know you better than I know anyone, and you were right when you told me you have flaws." Her eyes widen, and I can't help smiling as I continue. "You never remember to fold the clothes in the dryer. You always kick off your shoes in the middle of the living room. And, as you demonstrated tonight, you're *always* late."

She's glaring at me now, but there's no heat behind it. "Well, *you* yell at the TV as if football players can actually hear you."

I chuckle. God, I love her.

"The point is, I don't just accept all of that about you, I love all of your quirks."

"Ooh, tell me more about these quirks," she says.

My cheeks ache from smiling. This wasn't meant to be a back-and-forth conversation, but I don't care. I'll talk to her all night about how great she is as long as she says yes to my question in the end.

"You make the best chocolate chip cookies in the world. And you wrinkle your nose when you read. Your smile brightens my entire life, and I want to spend the rest of that life *with* you." At this point, I slide out of my chair and onto one knee, still holding her left hand in mine.

I pull the ring box out of my pocket. "Kaylee Martin, for all the reasons I just listed and about a million more, will you marry me?"

Tears shine in her eyes as I open the box, but she

doesn't even look at the princess-cut diamond ring. Her eyes are locked on to mine, shining love upon me as she says the only word I want to hear.

"Yes!"

I slide the ring onto her finger, rise to my feet, and pull her into my arms, just as the restaurant breaks out in applause.

Thanks for reading! What's next?

**Falling for Love:** Jack Dare's story!

Want more of Kaylee and Tristan? Get an exclusive
**bonus epilogue** by going **HERE!**
dl.bookfunnel.com/sqvcbsl34v

If you loved **Falling for Real**, check out
**The Kingston Family** series, starting with
**Just One Night!**

**Want even more Carly books?**

CARLY'S BOOKLIST by Series – visit:
https://www.carlyphillips.com/CPBooklist

Sign up for Carly's Newsletter:
https://www.carlyphillips.com/CPNewsletter

Join Carly Phillips' Readers Lounge on Facebook:
https://www.carlyphillips.com/CarlysCorner

Carly on Facebook:
https://www.carlyphillips.com/CPFanpage

Carly on Instagram:
https://www.carlyphillips.com/CPInstagram

# Carly's Booklist

*newest series listed first*

## The Dare to Fall Series

Book 1: Falling for Trouble (Rainey Dare & Lucas Carras)

Book 2: Falling for Real (Kaylee Martin & Tristan Hayes)

Book 3: Falling for Love (Sophie Monroe & Jack Dare)

## The Sterling Family

Book 1: Just One More Moment (Remington Sterling & Raven Walsh)

Book 2: Just One More Dare (Dex Kingston & Samantha Dare)

Book 3: Just One More Mistletoe (Max Corbin & Brandy Bloom)

Book 4: Just One More Temptation (Fallon Sterling & Noah Powers)

Book 5: Just One More Affair (Jared Sterling & Charlotte Kendall)

Book 6: Just One More Time (Aiden Sterling & Brooke Snyder)

Book 7: Just One More Date (Leo Watson & Camille Hendricks)

**The Dirty Dares**

Book 1: Just One Dare (Aurora Kingston & Nick Dare)

Book 2: Just One Kiss (Jade Dare & Knox Sinclair)

Book 3: Just One Taste (Asher Dare & Nicolette Bettencourt)

Book 4: Just One Fling (Harrison Dare & Winter Capwell)

Book 5: Just One Tease (Zach Dare & Hadley Stevens)

Novella: Just One Summer (Maddox James & Gabriella Davenport)

**The Kingston Family**

Book 1: Just One Night (Linc Kingston & Jordan Greene)

Book 2: Just One Scandal (Chloe Kingston & Beck Daniels)

Book 3: Just One Chance (Xander Kingston & Sasha Keaton)

Book 4: Just One Spark (Dash Kingston & Cassidy Forrester)

Just Another Spark – Short Story (Dash & Cassidy revisited)

Novella: Just One Wish (Axel Forrester & Tara Stillman)

## Dare Nation

Book 1: Dare to Resist (Austin Prescott &
Quinn Stone)
Book 2: Dare to Tempt (Damon Prescott &
Evie Wolfe)
Book 3: Dare to Play (Jaxon Prescott & Macy Walker)
Book 4: Dare to Stay (Brandon Prescott &
Willow James)
Novella: Dare to Tease (Hudson Northfield &
Brianne Prescott)

## The Sexy Series

Book 1: More Than Sexy (Jason Dare &
Faith Lancaster)
Book 2: Twice As Sexy (Tanner Grayson &
Scarlett Davis)
Book 3: Better Than Sexy (Landon Bennett &
Vivienne Clark)
Novella: Always Sexy (Shane Warden & Amber Davis)

## The Knight Brothers

Book 1: Take Me Again (Sebastian Knight &
Ashley Easton)
Novella: Take The Bride (Sierra Knight &
Ryder Hammond)
Book 2: Take Me Down (Parker Knight &
Emily Stevens)
Book 3: Dare Me Tonight (Ethan Knight &

Sienna Dare)

Take Me Now – Short Story (Harper Stevens &
Matt Banks)

**The New York Dares**
Book 1: Dare to Surrender (Gabe Dare &
Isabelle Masters)
Book 2: Dare to Submit (Decklan Dare &
Amanda Collins)
Book 3: Dare to Seduce (Max Savage & Lucy Dare)

**Dare to Love Series**
Book 1: Dare to Love (Ian Dare & Riley Taylor)
Book 2: Dare to Desire (Alex Dare & Madison Evans)
Book 3: Dare to Touch (Dylan Rhodes & Olivia Dare)
Book 4: Dare to Hold (Scott Dare & Meg Thompson)
Book 5: Dare to Rock (Avery Dare & Grey Kingston)
Book 6: Dare to Take (Tyler Dare & Ella Shaw)
A Very Dare Christmas – Short Story (Ian &
Riley revisited)

**Billionaire Bad Boys**
Book 1: Going Down Easy (Kaden Barnes &
Lexie Parker)
Book 2: Going Down Fast (Lucas Monroe &
Maxie Sullivan)
Book 3: Going Down Hard (Derek West &
Cassie Storms)

Book 4: Going In Deep (Julian Dane &
Kendall Parker)
Going Down Again – Short Story (Kade &
Lexie revisited)

**Bodyguard Bad Boys**
Book 1: Rock Me (Ben Hollander &
Summer Michelle)
Book 2: Tempt Me (Austin Rhodes & Mia Atwood)
Novella: His To Protect (Talia Shaw & Shane Landon)

**Serendipity Series**
Book 1: Serendipity (Ethan Barron &
Faith Harrington)
Book 2: Kismet (Lissa Gardelli & Trevor Dane)
Book 3: Destiny (Nash Barron & Kelly Moss)
Book 4: Fated (Kate Andrews & Nick Mancini)
Book 5: Karma (Dare Barron & Liza McKnight)

**Serendipity's Finest**
Book 1: Perfect Fit (Michael Marsden & Cara Hartley)
Book 2: Perfect Fling (Erin Marsden & Cole Sanders)
Book 3: Perfect Together (Sam Marsden &
Nicole Farnsworth)
Book 4: Perfect Strangers (Alexa Collins &
Luke Thompson)

**Hot Heroes Series**

Book 1: Touch You Now (Halley Ward & Kane Harmon)

Book 2: Hold You Now (Phoebe Ward & Jake Nichols)

Book 3: Need You Now (Juliette Collins & Braden Clark)

Book 4: Want You Now (Andi Harmon & Kyle Davenport)

**The Chandler Brothers**

Book 1: The Bachelor (Roman Chandler & Charlotte Bronson)

Book 2: The Playboy (Rick Chandler & Kendall Sutton)

Book 3: The Heartbreaker (Chase Chandler & Sloane Carlisle)

**The Lucky Series**

Book 1: Lucky Charm (Derek Corwin & Gabrielle Donovan)

Book 2: Lucky Streak (Mike Corwin & Amber Rose Brennan)

Book 3: Lucky Break (Jason Corwin & Lauren Perkins)

## Costas Sisters

Book 1: Under the Boardwalk (Ariana Costas &
Quinn Donovan)
Book 2: Summer of Love (Zoe Costas &
Ryan Baldwin)

## Ty and Hunter

Book 1: Cross My Heart (Lilly Dumont & Ty Benson)
Book 2: Sealed with a Kiss (Molly Gifford &
Daniel Hunter)

## The Hot Zone

Book 1: Hot Stuff (Annabelle Jordan &
Brandon Vaughn)
Book 2: Hot Number (Micki Jordan & Damian Fuller)
Book 3: Hot Item (Sophie Jordan & Riley Nash)
Book 4: Hot Property (Amy Stone & John Roper)

## The Simply Series

Book 1: Simply Sinful (Kayla Luck &
Kane McDermott)
Book 2: Simply Scandalous (Catherine Luck &
Logan Montgomery)
Book 3: Simply Sensual (Ben Callahan &
Grace Montgomery)
Book 4: Body Heat (Jake Lowell & Brianne Nelson)
Book 5: Simply Sexy (Rina Lowell & Colin Lyons)

**The Most Eligible Bachelor Series**
Book 1: Kiss Me if You Can (Sam Cooper &
Lexie Davis)
Book 2: Love Me If You Dare (Rafe Mancuso &
Sara Rios)

**Carly Classics**
Book 1: The Right Choice (Carly Wexler &
Mike Novak)
Book 2: Perfect Partners (Chelsie Russell &
Griffin Stuart)
Book 3: Unexpected Chances (Dylan North &
Holly Evans)
Book 4: Worthy of Love (Kevin Manning &
Nikki Welles)

# About the Author

Carly Phillips is the *NY Times*, *Wall Street Journal*, and *USA Today* bestselling author of over eighty sexy contemporary romances featuring hot men, strong women, and the emotionally compelling stories her readers have come to expect and love. She is happily married to her college sweetheart and lives outside New York City. She is the mother of two adult daughters and a Havanese puppy who stars on her social media and newsletter. Visit her website: www.carly phillips.com.